CYAN

MAGENTA

YELLOW

BLACK

Cyan Magenta Yellow Black

A NOVEL

KEVIN FENTON

BLACK LAWRENCE PRESS

Black Lawrence Press

Executive Editor: Diane Goettel
Book Cover and Interior Design: Zoe Norvell

"Nothing is Perfect except the light falling on imperfection," from Resort And Other Poems by Patricia Hampl. Copyright © 1983 by Patricia Hampl. Used by permission of HarperCollins Publishers.

ISBN: 978-1-62557-1-960

Published 2025 by Black Lawrence Press.
Printed in the United States.

To Ellen

*And to everyone who found themselves hanging out on
Grand Avenue in the early 90s.*

ACKNOWLEDGEMENTS

These people read somewhat less satisfying versions of this book so you can read what I hope is a very satisfying version of it: Ellen Shaffer, Cheri Johnson, Michael Walsh, Daryl Lanz, Jon Spayde, Amanda Fields, Joe Isaak, and Andria Williams. For their generosity and insight, I am forever grateful.

And special thanks to Diane Goettel and Black Lawrence Press. When I told people in the writing world that Black Lawrence was publishing my book they invariably said, "Oh, they're really good." They really are.

Parts of this book have appeared, in different forms, in *Ploughshares* and *Shenandoah*.

Love for the Wet Air
and the Soft Gray Sky

1

No one was having a good day. It was December in Minnesota in 1993 and we were all at a stage in our life where our therapist thought we might be less loser-like if we met late Monday morning. Late morning, because early morning wasn't an option for some of us—because some of us couldn't keep ourselves from loitering in the hours past midnight. But it had to be Monday morning because the point of this meeting was to inflect the remainder of the week. We should have been in twelve-step programs, but we lacked the required focus to be alcoholics. We should have had families but we misplaced them or never formed them or rejected them as worse than loneliness.

It was December in Minnesota, which is to say that it had snowed last night—a wet, tenuous snow—and as I walked to group I proceeded carefully over the silvery scraped sidewalks and less carefully over the white unshoveled ones.

And, if my fellow group members were like me, and they were, they were intermittently filled with love for the wet air and the soft gray sky and the brick buildings and the other things which were not our agitated egos and our adhesive couches. They maybe loved the buildings most: the chocolate brick, the cinnamon brick, the ginger brick, the cardamom brick. We loved the bricks because they reminded us of spices and spices reminded us of love. We relied on the world to poke through our self-involvement a little bit. Walks improved us. Walks improved us so much they were more or less prescribed to us. Walks dissipated our sticky emotional weathers, our condensing sadnesses, our near tears, our overcast silences, our staticky thrashings—whatever it is that scrapes and worries in us so at the end of the day we aren't sure we've actually lived. A little wind on our necks, a small bright thing in our vision: a neon scrawl on a diner, a purple serif of a bloom in a florist window. These perforations of the self were more important to us than they were to most people. We had already been too cooked by whatever silent scream constituted our inner lives and brought us here. We loved the world because it was not us.

Which is not to say that we were not bastards because we were. We were drunk drivers, no-call-no-shows, throwers of tantrums; our answering machines were abysses where our loved ones' good intentions went to die. We were whiners, shirkers, blamers, rationalizers, ranters, procrastinators, grudge-holders, chronics, hair-pullers, liars, sad sacks, histrionics, and saboteurs. We caused bad days. We invented addictions. We were occasionally just stupid.

But enough about my friends. It was December in Minnesota which meant that not having replaced the gloves I had lost last year had its tiny consequences, as the wind howled as if across an opened pop bottle; the flesh on my hands pinkened and chapped.

A young woman approaching me smiled. Winter for her was as gentle as a photograph. The wind was at her back.

A Dunn Brothers coffee cup bounced along the boulevard, making little divots in the snow. The wind chapped my ears, too. I really needed to get a hat. I had money now, the non-compete I signed when I left the agency provided for that, but I didn't have income. The two things feel very different. It's a feeling that leads you to not quite get around to buying hats or replacing gloves. I knew that, before this time next week, I should buy Christmas presents for at least some of the people I was about to see, but I didn't want to buy them or do much of anything. Per some recent suggestions, I put one foot after another and breathed deeply.

2

Irv Shilton patiently approaches me. Usually he gets my approval. Sometimes he doesn't.

I stand in a chilled, humming, high-ceilinged, gray-aired factory. Glistening mugs slide toward me on a conveyer belt. They are illuminated in a cone of nicotine-yellow light from an overhead bulb. If I were in charge, I would use white lights, more diffusely, with a light table under, but I am not in charge here. I am the opposite of in charge.

I pick up the advancing mugs and inspect them. Because the light's from a single source, it casts shadows. I flip the mug and read it.

Irv's Shriners club is having a dinner to celebrate his fifty years of service to the Shriners. They've created these mugs to honor him: an eagle in a blue oval teeters on a cameo of Irv's jowly smiling fez-topped face, which rests on a little scroll in some ludicrously serifed Old English Type.

Irv lives in a town like my town or, rather, like the town I grew up in. Towns, actually. First the farm town of New Luxembourg, Minnesota and then, in high school, after my dad died, Mom and I moved to the river town of Minnisapa. New Luxembourg had a creamery and two bars and gossip. Minnisapa was large enough to have its own paper and radio station. The paper treated preposterously large vegetables as news. The radio station treated polka as popular music. I live in Saint Paul now, and it's not a town at all but a city, although just barely.

I know everything that's wrong with these mugs: the half tone is too detailed for such a coarse screen so the ink clumps, giving Irv what appear to be blackheads; the design is some sort of totem pole to the god of clichés.

Then there is the kerning: a design teacher once told me that I should imagine that the space between letters held water and that each space should hold the same amount of water and that I should nudge and nudge and nudge letters microns of an inch left or right until I had achieved this balance which, when seen by the untrained eye, both calms and animates. Whoever cut the screens for Irv Shilton's image didn't attend this lecture. The "S" is practically groping the "h." The "i" looks like it's hoping someone will ask it to dance.

I realize that I have been standing for a couple of hours, watching mugs approach. My feet and legs have thickened.

I look at a sweet well-intended commemorative mug and see nothing but gaps and tensions.

In my previous job, nothing like this would have gotten anywhere near me. Six months ago, I had my name on the door of a small but highly creative, well, pretty creative, advertising agency. I had the strange title of executive art director. Every morning, I walked into offices made of artful bricks and elegant sunlight. I had a staff of three art directors and two writers. To create a single ad, we filled the wall with ideas. Each idea was subject to a friendly inquisition before it even left the door. And then when the ads were produced, the copy was sent to typographers who explored the spaces between the letters with the delicacy of brain surgeons.

Here, now, in this chilled space, I shatter the bad mugs in a cardboard box on the floor.

I see a smudge, I lift and smash the offending mug.

I see a heat pimple; I look down; I see shards; I shatter the pimpled mug and see more shards.

The mugs continue to approach me at a pace that is too slow and too fast.

The assembly line is as inconsiderate as a dream.

I place the good mugs on another conveyor belt, where they disappear behind a flap, into a kiln. Heat wisps out.

When Irv Shilton sees his mugs, when they are handed out to his friends, when his friends toast him in a church basement while they sit on beige folding chairs around chipped brown tables rimmed with gray metal, when he smells cheap coffee or steamed chicken, when he fights the lullaby of air that's a little too warm, when he struggles to listen to speeches in the clanging cluttered acoustics of those big hard-walled places, Irv will fight back tears. He will know how rich his life has been.

Me, my life? Not so much. I'm working here today, in this factory, because my therapist and I both agreed I needed to get out of my apartment.

*　　*　　*

After this shift is over, I will return to my apartment. I view it as a bit of a come-down, but 90% of the world would consider it a dream of spaciousness and luxury.

I live in a one-bedroom apartment on Grand Avenue in Saint Paul, in one of the brick apartment buildings built right before the modernists gave every contractor permission to be cheap and ugly.

Today, I work here. I never thought I would be in a factory, working this shift. I thought I was done with drone work and lonely apartments. I thought that once I got through to Jay Latir, from the pay phone on the corner of University and Central, between busses, on the way to the Sparkle Dry Cleaners, so many years ago, the dismal, drudging, impoverished part of my life was over. I thought that I had forever joined the happy middle class legions who get to think a little at work and get to spend a little when they are not working.

The dry cleaners was how I had put myself through art school. I hated that dungeony, steaming, kerosene-smelling, whirring, Dickensian chemical world. I will tell you this about Dickensian, it lacks something as an actual lifestyle choice. The problem wasn't that I was bad at dry cleaning. What's there to be bad at? You wait at the bottom of the chute for the thump of worn clothes, softened by their time against human skin, you sort loads, you pre-treat them, you toss them in the machines, you smack release-valves on the big chemical-sloshing machines when they get stuck, you hang the warm clothes; you shoot the stains out with a steam gun. This last bit required a deft touch, but I was pretty good at it.

But I hated being broke. I hated having a crap red Capri that festered outside my apartment like some sacrifice to the god of entropy. I hated bringing home grocery bags full of three-for-a-dollar mac and cheese. The macaroni was so pale, it was Caucasian. The cheese was vaguely industrial. I hated the strangers who, through some weird game of musical roommates, now shared my apartment and played heavy metal albums at all hours.

When the Capri finally broke down for good, I started to despise buses, in that special way that entitled assholes like me despise the vulnerable and the unfortunate. I hated how buses were as breathy and tender as whales, the way their pneumatics would sigh when they would stop and gather us up, the way they were illuminated and floating and filled with people looking straight ahead. I hated the way bus riders' sadness seemed to diffuse into the air in front of them.

As the school year ticked into summer and summer ticked into fall, I did not return to school, and for the first time in sixteen years I did not buy new art supplies. I was tired of telling people what I did.

"I work in a dry cleaner but . . ." Every day my job hardened into who I was. Every day, the recession of the early '80s loitered like some not-quite-friend who would not quite leave. Of course, my friends weren't getting jobs either but that just made our parties more dismal.

I hated the weekly calls to my mom because I would launch into my complaint about the dry cleaners and buses and mac and cheese and a crap apartment and she would remind me that I had a job and I had food and in her world that was something. She had grown up in the depression in the small Minnesota farm town where I was born. She had grown up in a world where, if a bad-smelling man shows up at your door, a man you called a "hobo" not a homeless man, you asked the stranger to wait on the porch and then you cooked him a fried egg sandwich and said grace with him. In her world, manners and gratefulness were gods and everything went wrong when we stopped meaning it when we gave thanks for our food.

In the days of crap transportation and crap shelter and crap work, I came to the simple enough realization that my art required money. Of course, everything requires money; a serious artist has to buy his mac and cheese so he can eat; he has to eat so can smear his profundities on some canvas. But in the case of the serious artist, the money is metabolized into things that matter. This gave the bastards who created serious art a claim on a certain self-righteousness, which in my art school naturally created tension between the fine artists and the designers. Well, tension in that they thought we were fascists and we wished they wouldn't think that, especially since the fascism wasn't going so well at the moment for me, what with the underemployment in the Victorian cellar and the microwaved diet.

It sucks when the people who call you a fascist have a point. When our history of design class was shown an Italian poster from the late '30s, the thing that stuck with me was how the "s" had been so deftly reduced to a single slash. I didn't want to see what has become obvious: that both designers and fascists are minimalists, are editors, are distillers, are eliminators of impurities. It's no accident that the Nazis had a good logo.

It wasn't like fine art was above criticism: namely, its worldview left a few things out. Such as, you know, joy. For his senior project, my Minnisapa friend Craig Wall did these paintings of agonized, pseudo-woodcut faces with bodies that were all stigmata and tripe. I remember thinking, "You grew up in Minnisapa, for chrissake! Are your friends really this bummed out all the time? Couldn't they maybe cheer up a little? Like play some Twister or dance to some Dave Clark Five records?" When I pointed this out to him, he just gave me the shrug you give the clueless. Of course, since then a life with guts exposed, a life where it's hard to summon the will to move, a life where nothing promises joy, has seemed a little more plausible.

Ultimately, there was one big difference I couldn't deny between the fine artists and people like me. What I do requires money in a way that goes far beyond being able to afford food and paint. What I do requires the hum and fizz and confidence of money. What I do requires eight-color Heidelberg presses and 4,000-square-foot photography studios with huge angelic windows and nubile assistants and offices that throb with coolness and cities planted with billboards and landscapes planted with towers that beam dancing light to ten million television sets in eight million homes.

And all of this—the months filled with crap, disappointment and frustration—explains why when Jay Latir finally said, "You're hired, buddy," I danced at the payphone, stone cold sober, and that next day I bought a Big Chief notebook and ten new pencils.

*   *   *

The foreman walks from line to line, nodding, and someone flicks a switch and each line quiets and stops. The quiet surprises me. My sense of how a shift ends was entirely based on Flintstone reruns, where the bird squawks and Fred dismounts the dinosaur which had been called into service as a crane.

I must have seemed confused. The foreman motions me toward the lit break room. The light, not straining to complete any tasks, seems to relax. In the break room, there are celebrity magazines, both neglected and pawed, with Jeff Goldblum and Nicole Kidman on them.

The people here are silent. I'm not sure how they wound up here, but then they are not sure how I wound up here. They are silent as if life is an interrogation and they are taking the fifth: a thick woman with a potatoey face and hair that appears to be held in a hairnet, although it isn't. Her cigarette seems to burn with her anger. A round-eyed woman who seems Hispanic. She looks down at the floor. They are horrible at small talk.

Small talk now seems like a miracle and I miss it like a friend. No one is going on about some sitcom, no one is repeating lines, no one is borrowing effervescences from something they saw on TV: no Homer Simpsons, no Jerry Seinfelds, no guys at actual copiers imitating the copier guy on SNL imitating guys at copiers. There isn't the usual litany of restaurant reviews and art house movies dropped as credentials. The people who work here don't spend time establishing that they are more interesting than their at-work selves appear to be. What did you do on the weekend? I worked in places where you worried about the answer to that question in the way my parents worried about what they would say to Saint Peter in heaven. The answer to the question would define you. But here nobody's talking. I take that personally.

A kid—maybe 19—stands next to the vending machine. I see him in profile and he's ridiculously skinny. The vending machine grinds and releases something which then, a half beat later, thuds.

I carry on a hypothetical monologue about these new vending machines:

"What's with the design of these things? What were they thinking? Let's give each candy a little special code because it would be impossible to just point and pull. Then let's have the little spiral holder spin so you have to wait for it. Then the candy bar should plummet from a great height. Yes, it's important that the cinnamon roll plummet. Soften it up some. Then you need to stick your hand through this bar that kind of catches on your knuckles." I know better than to say this to this crowd.

Instead, I say, because, you know, it wouldn't kill me to break the ice: "I once got really mad at a vending machine. And smacked it with my hand. It dropped one of everything."

There's no reaction, except a slight deepening of disgust and distance on the faces of the two women, as if they have further resolved not to talk to me.

The kid walks over from the vending machine. He's unwrapping a Hostess pie. The sibilance of the ripping plastic is a little too loud. This gangly kid has an odd angular confidence; he moves like he learned how to walk by watching cartoons. He speaks to the two women.

"What's up, Steph?" She says, "the usual" to him in a way that, if it isn't exactly cheerful, suggests he might understand her discomfort.

"You Nice." He says to the round-faced woman. Her name must be Eunice. She smiles.

Then he nods at me. He is wearing a stocking cap, even though we're inside, and a t-shirt with a skeleton playing the banjo. His coolness is tentative, he's not used to it being public. He's used to an easy, familiar crowd: Steph and Eunice. He nods briskly at me, dude to dude, a truce of a nod.

His fruit pie has that thin wrapper: bright white and enticing in a way that reminds me of sugar, streaked with two bands of red that I think are meant to invoke the Coke wave.

"Did you ever see the Marvel comic book ads for those in the '70s?"

"Nope."

"They have like Captain America or the Daredevil fight crime by giving the bad guys Hostess Fruit Pies. They'd say things like, 'Better a Hostess Fruit Pie than the fruits of crime.'"

"Nope." He shakes his head and makes eye contact with bitter Steph. They act like I'm hallucinating and they are patronizing me.

"They were some weird ads," I say, as if confirming my sense of reality.

He did not see the ads. My guess is that he may have read a few comic books and taken a graphic arts course in high school and realized he had a little talent at a vaguely cool thing. He did not run into the room as a five-year-old and stand, transfixed, in front of the TV when commercials came on. The kid in the banjo-playing skeleton t-shirt did not cover one wall of his boyhood room with a galaxy of red, green and blue Spirograph patterns. He did not take Polaroids of his etch-a-sketch drawings. He did not collect baseball cards to savor the pleasures of the typography and color theory long before he realized that such things as typography and color theory could be studied; he did not cadge old issues of *Sport* magazine from friends' uncles so he could absorb the tobacco-and-cream smell of the 1950s' paper and the testimonials for Brylcreem and Aqua Velva featuring line-drawn athletes with crew cut heads like exclamation marks. He did not stare at the strange appearance of a war bonneted Indian Chief on his dad's Red Man chewing tobacco and he did not examine the Copenhagen chewing tobacco tins with the embossed tin lids and wonder how those images were deposited on that paper or stamped into that metal or how the blue plastic of Vicks vapor rub became blue. His room wasn't arrayed with neat galleries of stamps and at-attention formations of army men and showrooms of Hot Wheels cars.

The kid in the skeleton t-shirt did not cajole his teacher into letting him create a sixth-grade newspaper on fragrant purple mimeos which he cranked out himself and inhaled when they appeared, and he did not take it upon himself to create a scout troop paper on a strange long-since obsolete printing gel; he did not design his own merit badges. The cartoon kid in the cartoon t-shirt did not collect and index comic books; he didn't live vicariously through their punches of meaning. The kid did not smell paste and the special plastic fragrance of encyclopedia binding and the nostalgic toxins of mimeo fluid and markers and think of home.

As the kid in the skeleton shirt moved from a farm town to a larger town where he knew no one, he did not spend that first lonely summer looking up old television shows in TV trivia books, shows he had never seen, and making up episodes and creating graphics and promos. The kid in the skeleton shirt did not know that *Pride of the Family*, a half-hour sitcom starring Paul Hartman as the head of an advertising department for a local paper, ran just over a year in the early fifties. He did not know that *Szysznyk* starring Ned Beatty as a twenty-seven-year Marine Corps veteran who became the supervisor of the Northeast Community Center in Washington, D.C. "also featured Barry Miller as Fortwengler." He was not so amused by the name Fortwengler that he made up a show about Fortwengler, making the logo a jaunty scarf of text, like the type on a pennant.

In high school the kid in the skeleton shirt did not go to movies in Minnisapa, Minnesota with his tentatively made new friends and seethe through their wise guy yammering. He did not risk being seen as a loser by going to movies alone simply because he loved watching them. He was not amazed, when he moved from a small town without a movie theater to a bigger town with three at the idea of being able to walk to a building constructed for no other purpose than to showcase an image: he did not love the amnesia of the dark, the luminescent screen, the quick intimacy of the movie trailers. Skeleton banjo boy did not come to the Twin Cities after high school to study film-making, and then realize that he would never make films because when he had stood behind the camera he found that film was too suffused with the actual and the accidental, too crowded and random, too gratingly collaborative. He did not then gravitate to graphic design, attracted by its discipline and limits—the way type could be slid 1/64th of an inch, the way a serif could be delicately shaved, the way a good poster could be the world's most subtle machine, the way colors and shapes and images could be selected so that they were a vivid and intelligent and efficient thing in a half-assed, first-draft, mumbling, misunderstood, shy, staticky and often stupid world.

No, that was me.

Graphics was what I loved. Graphics, not art with its viscera of purely personal emotion showing; but pictures with the pulse of entertainment and salesmanship. Graphics was the organizing principle of every one of my Christmas lists—and I was such a selfish little brat, I actually made and shared them and sent my mom off in search of 64 pack crayons and Big Chief tablets and #2 pencils and translucent green pencil sharpeners and wooden rulers with golden edges and the Broadway Boogie Woogie of a Lego set. And then as I grew older every birthday and Christmas was a requisitioning of Letraset letters and X-Acto knives and drawing boards and anatomical models and layout markers and foam core. Graphics was what I loved and what I pursued as less a man than permanent boy until my fiancée broke it off and then I lost my job because I was a ranting fuck-up and whenever I looked at what I had once loved—a clever headline, a colorful page—it made me sick and in America in 1993, you can't not see the designed world everywhere you look. Those things don't quite make me sick anymore and they don't quite make me happy like they used to, either. Who the hell has complex feelings about kerning, about PMS colors, about drop shadows? I liked the world a little better when design made me sick. I liked the world better when I hated something other than myself.

*   *   *

My shrink calls this—this loitering in a nothing life, this loveless, jobless lostness of the past months—depression, insists that it's a disease—or more accurately, insists that I am feeling a grief that will harden into depression if I don't get off my butt. We call my shrink Sergeant Serenity. To me, this feeling that punishes and deflates me feels like nothing more or less than the realization that I have loved the wrong things. It is the realization that, when the woman I loved suffered in lonely sadness on our couch, I played with colors. It is the realization that even now, when I know that what I love is stupid, that I can't stop loving it. I look at that Irv Shilton mug and I still want it to be set in a better font. I can't help any of this but that doesn't mean it's not a sin. We think that love is a deep emotion, but my love is shallow as ink. In such a case, spending weeks on one's couch is the only plausible thing to do and in those hours a smudged, unsatisfactory sadness enters you the way wind and fallen leaves enter an abandoned building; there's this pressure behind your eyes that never quite becomes tears, because tears are too clean and cleansing, because tears are too proactive and can do, because tears assume at least a little self-love, a sense that "it is sad that this is happening to me." There's really nothing sad about my sadness. I deserve it. Sick of my mind, my sadness drifts into my hollow gut and limp hands and heavy legs.

I am here at this factory to simply get moving.

3

The foreman approaches me. I sense him coming and, when I look up, he motions me to his office. We walk single file, me behind him. His shoulders give me no clues. As he sits down, he lights up a cigarette. I'm not sure he's supposed to. He leans forward with his hands on his knees and his cigarette bobbing like the beak of a bird. He tightens up his mouth, which pulls up his gelatinous red beard. He looks at me:

"You've got a good eye and you seem pretty steady."

"Thanks."

"Would you be interested in coming on full time? We can use the help."

I hadn't expected this.

"I'm not sure. Things are kind of in flux right now." I feel awful as I say this because what I really mean is "no." And my foreman's the essence of a guy trying to do his job.

"That's why people work temp," he says. He takes a drag on his cigarette. "I just make the offer, because sometimes they want something more permanent."

I cannot tell him: you are an exercise from my therapist, you are a cautionary tale, you were never a serious option. "Thanks for thinking of me," I say, and feel like a jerk.

If I weren't such a hypocrite, being here in this factory wouldn't be a problem. I talk a good game about all work being noble. At the occasional brainstorm, back in my former life where we were discussing how to convince a working-class audience to buy something, at one of those meetings where someone invariably uses the phrase "Joe Six-Pack," as if that is all the insight we would need, I had been known to be contrary. I've been known to say, "Just because these guys don't have college degrees doesn't mean they're stupid."

Maybe because I grew up in New Luxembourg—we moved to Minnisapa when I was between ninth and tenth grade—I would think of myself as working class. After all, my mom worked as a nurse and all my uncles were farmers and most of my friends were farm kids, which meant that I knew a lot of people who handled shit now and then and who used their muscles to lift and whose feet were sore at the end of the day.

But, as a nurse, Mom watched the interaction of drugs and the evolution of symptoms in people who might die before the day was out and the New Luxembourg farmers looked at fields and weather and machinery and livestock and inventories and noticed whatever it is that threatens a farm.

And I was also the son of a math teacher in New Luxembourg's small Catholic school. My dad yearned for a perfect, platonic exploration of the elegances of Euclidean geometry and algebra. He was a good teacher, a reluctant but competent enough disciplinarian, who both loved his students and hated their shrugging indifference. But I think he most loved inhabiting, for however many hours a day, the school building, where proofs and insights and resolutions might happen, where students and the nuns and even the priest chimed "Mr. Einwald" as if he were Aristotle's representative in our little town.

When Saint Agnes school failed, he crumbled. He did not know what he was when he was not walking the halls of Saint Agnes, when he was not the man who deftly deposited the equations on the blackboard; when he was not standing tall and serene in the barely contained riot that was a high school hallway; when a roomful of students was not focused, however indifferently, on him; when he was not marking and grading; when the nuns addressed him with the almost flirtatious respect they reserved for priests. Not wanting us to move, he took a job driving a bulk truck that gathered the farmers' milk. He died of a heart attack within six months.

So, yeah, I have some working class sympathies. But no one in my family was spending their days standing at the end of an assembly line, either. I'm not telling anyone about this temp gig.

4

I return to my post. Other mugs, ecstatic with clip art and exclamation marks within pointless quotation marks, advance toward me: Dupree's Feeds— "The Feed You Need, The Service You Want!"; Tim and Tom's Plumbing— "There when you're feeling Flush!"; and then Saint Irene Circle— "Ask about our Christmas Recipe Book!" I'd forgotten about church circles, groups of ladies from a parish who make quilts and jams and put on charity dinners. I discover the mugs' imperfections and inflict violence upon them. I'm pretty sure I have to pee, as the mugs continue to stream toward me, but I haven't asked how you might do this.

The shift ends. When I arrive at the urinal, I focus on the greenish rust and the droplets of condensed water on the flushing mechanism and sort of push with my bladder and realize that I am just anxious. I may not need to pee, after all, so I'm just a guy standing there with his dick out. Because it's the shift's end, other men will soon appear and, as I think this, I hear the door swing open and an eruption of voices that quiets when the door sighs and slams. The banjo-playing-skeleton guy materializes at the urinal one over from me. He says, "Hey" and keeps looking forward, as do I.

He unzips and pisses with an assurance I normally associate with James Bond.

God, in his mercy, allows me to release a middling stream and I aim it at the water pooled in the bottom of the urinal so that it makes a sound. It is somehow important that Banjo Boy knows that I am, in fact, peeing.

Banjo boy, staring at his portion of wall, speaks. "This isn't your normal gig, right?"

I stare at my portion of wall and say, "Yeah, right. How'd you know?"

His stream stops. He zips and turns to me and nods toward the Brooks Brothers logo on my oxford shirt. "Not a lot of Ralph Lauren around here."

I don't correct him.

"I suppose not," I say. He's taken a few steps toward what I assume is the door. No, the sink. Water gushes then stops, a towel scrolls violently out of one of those machines.

I shake my dick and zip up. When I turn, he's at the door.

"Did you work on the Irv Shilton mug?"

"Yeah, I did."

"I wasn't really happy with that," he admits.

"That half-tone they provided. There's only so much you can do with that in a silk screen."

"Yeah, you're right. I tried to add some other stuff so I don't have to make it too big."

"Yeah, it worked pretty well." The kid actually acknowledged he didn't think the design worked. Why was I being such a wuss? Why couldn't I just tell him, maybe simplify the type a little and run it over and under the image so you can lose that hideous eagle. Me, and my big standards.

"Thanks," the kid says.

5

I grab my coat from the area provided for temps. I make yet another mental note to buy gloves. As I walk out the big double door, snow falls: angling in the air near me, drifting in the air in the distance. Snow animates the air and touches my face and accumulates on my head. Footprints, the oldest already filling with new flakes, lead to cars. At the cars, people—including my new buddy, and Steph—are still brushing off windshields. Except for those footsteps, the world is covered with snow as sparkling as diamonds and as pure as clouds. Exhaust steams around the cars. When Steph brushes the snow off her passenger's side window, she reveals Eunice, who turns and smiles at her. I get to my car and open the cold handle and crawl inside to search for my snow scraper like someone entering a cave. I then sit in the cold, cramped space of the front seat, start the car up, set the heater to high and start the defrost. I shiver.

When I get out to brush the windshield, Banjo Boy gives his headlights one last Jedi lightsaber swat to remove the snow that has caked over them. Their beams brighten. He yells, "Have a good one, buddy" as he gets in his car.

I yell, "You too, bud."

Snow in the air is happiness. Snow on the landscape is beauty. Snow on the roads is fear. I tense as I back up and pivot and leave the parking lot. I know the roads are slick beneath me. I know that stopping needs to be a slow tactful process, like waking an animal. I know that sudden braking will send me skating off the road or spinning into an intersection. I know that if I unconsciously go too fast, that if I fail to feel and understand my car's speed, that there will be nothing I can do but turn into the skid and hope it dissipates before anything is crunched or killed or stranded or embarrassed. The snow continues to fall, and the windshield wipers squeegee it away, and the defroster turns it into water. My shoulders tighten. The heater is loud and stern and competes with the puppyish oldies on the radio. I turn the radio off, so I'm not distracted. In the edges of my vision, I see homes lit for the holidays: white lights (almost too tasteful), motley lights (orange? really?), a huge Homer Simpson Santa, and then heart-stunning yards and windows full of all blue lights, then another with all green lights. Snow continues to perfect the world.

A stop light approaches. Green, then yellow, then red. Even though I started braking almost a half block from the light, I've touched the brakes too emphatically and the car begins to skate. I take my feet off the brake. The car shimmies, threatens to veer, but then, thankfully, loses its momentum. I tap the brake and the car rests, ten feet back from the crosswalk.

As I inch toward the intersection, Banjo Boy's goodbye—"Have a good one, bud"—stays with me, as does Eunice's smile. I miss leaving work and people wishing you a good night. I miss that sense that somehow you've all fought the good fight for another day, I miss the way that almost mundane good feeling softens the rest of night up a little bit. "Have a good one, bud." For years, as we have exited elevators, as we have walked to cars and bus stops, as we've dispersed into the thing that isn't quite a city but a metro area, we have been blessing each other.

I sit, at almost midnight, at an empty intersection, snow still falling, heading toward an apartment brimming with absences.

6

When I enter my apartment and flip on the light, I'm once again disappointed by inanimate objects: a sweatshirt I'd worn earlier rests on the futon in the precise shrug of a shape it assumed when I tossed it there. The answering machine does not blink. I've left out a single slice of Kraft Cheese, with the wrapper with the weirdly generous flap and the perfect yellow-orange color and the now muddy texture of the cheese. I toss it out. I throw my overcoat over a chair's back then let the rest of my clothes puddle where they fall on the floor. When I'm under the covers, I tug out the tiny "on" lever on my alarm, a sturdy analog model with the numbers set in Bodoni's thicks and thins. I'd selected the Bodoni because I wanted something brisk and human to look at when I awoke. I hold the clock almost as if I were a pitcher cradling and scrutinizing a baseball: its heft both calms me and energizes me. I return it to its sentry post and darken the room and resign my face to my pillow, which I embrace with a little more enthusiasm than is strictly becoming, so I have to move my face to breathe.

I try to sleep in the silence and absence. Driving on the snow-slicked roads has pushed more adrenalin through me than I thought. I pace into the living room. I turn on the TV, like a man rubbing a lamp in the hope of some change in the situation, and release Conan

O'Brien: he seems both reptilian and nice. Don't we all. He gets to talk
to a pretty girl, and I let the sounds and sights of this replace whatever
might otherwise have been in my head. During a commercial break,
I eat cereal which, despite years of R and D by the finest minds in the
carbohydrates industry and nationally televised 60 second promises,
fails to stay crunchy in milk. I'm okay with that, as I ingest the com-
forting sludge.

I fall asleep on the futon couch but before I slept I turned off the TV
because I hate waking to static, which always strikes my confounded
consciousness as a kind of panic and pain so I always lurch toward
the TV, half awake, and turn it off before I realize that I am not rescu-
ing another being from chaos but just turning off a machine.

 With the TV off, I lay a few minutes with my limping, lazy—and,
finally, mercifully—dissolving thoughts.

EMILY

I whispered to Gertie that I was going to check her, and she nodded sweetly, as she does, and I pulled back the covers and saw the poop on the blue absorbent pads we put under her. I grab a new pad from her bedside, wet a towel with warm water, and spray some sweet-smelling soap into it. I roll her over gently, pull out the blue pads—they're a wrapper now—and throw the package out. She starts to move, as if to roll back. I hold her against the bed rail. "You'll need to stay there, while I wipe you." I am tired and my feet are sore, I just lean over her for a little while. She smiles.

"You didn't fuck with her, did you?" her roommate squawks.

"No, Audie, I didn't. I just cleaned her up."

"You better not fuck with her."

"I won't Audie," I say.

I turn the lights out on Gertie and Audie. Two women, two lives, two strategies.

The lights are down, except for the pool of light around the nurses' desk. Cyndy, R.N., petite, pretty, slightly too upbeat for her own good, is finishing up charting. "You going to join us for a drink after?" she asks.

"Not tonight," I say and lean against the nurse's station. I don't need to tell sweetness and light here—and she actually is sweet, the bitch—that some nights I just find our whole species *problematic*. We are monkeys who can write the occasional Edith Wharton novel. But mostly we are just monkeys.

I've worked twelve hours today—four as a perfume spritzer in a department store; eight here, in this nursing home—because I need the hours.

Home, I am too exhausted, too amped up from driving in the snow, too ambivalent about the Christmas lights which I should love but which just mock my glum aloneness, to go to bed. I make herbal tea.

You just know that someone somewhere is singing in some insipid voice, "All is calm. All is bright." Not so fast there, buddy. In here, in my tasteful yet thrifty single gal's apartment, all is neither calm nor bright.

I go worst case.

Worst case, in this case, is thinking about dentistry.

Worst case negates my otherwise not unbelievable affirmations. *I am competent. I am strong. I have read the most subtle sentences of our most subtle writers, and I have done what they dreamed of—I have listened to them over the decades for without minds like mine there is no literature.*

I am more than what has been done to me.

But when I sit here tonight, all I can think of is how I will soon be leaning back in that chair and giving up control as a man inflicts pain on my most vulnerable areas. There is on my refrigerator, affixed by a magnet with an image of a Paris street in the rain, a cheery reminder from my dentist. They are looking forward to my visit.

My visit is in two days. I like to be prepared.

PORTER

I'm parking my car and leaning over to grab the silver-wrapped pizza.
When I turn off the windshield wipers, the snow accumulates. When
I turn off my headlights, the darkness re-awakens. I wait for my eyes
to adjust. When I slam the door, snow shakes off the roof of my car.
The moon shines. The falling snow covers the walk to the house,
touches my bald head and catches in the tonsure of my gray hair. The
trees are shadows which cast shadows.

My therapist tells me, and everyone in our group, when we think
some past trauma is in the room with us, that *this* is not *that*. A sidewalk in Saint Paul is not a rice paddy. The man who raped my friend
when she was five is not the man who is dating her when she is twen-
ty-six. Our therapist tells us this but it is Christ who allows me to
believe that in Saint Paul, in 1993, the shadows do not hide Viet Cong.

But what if the darkness had already precipitated what you most
feared? What if, while walking one day, a mine catapulted into your
friend's chest and your friend became a mess you were wiping off
your face?

I know that I am delivering a pizza in one of the more affluent neighborhoods of Saint Paul. I know that I am near a Catholic university
named after the saint who doubted him, Thomas. This house is

rented by nice girls from the suburbs whose parents pay their rent.

I walk toward the light. A young woman looks out a window, eager for my arrival. The light has the beautiful amber softness of places of the middle class and of the places of women. Christmas lights glow behind and beside her.

I think of the magi, who brought luxurious gifts for a poor family. I joke to myself that Mary and Jesus and Joseph would have rather received a pizza. All believers seek to be the magi, seek to recognize the full implications of a seemingly humble light. We all seek to share our gifts, even if it is a medium sausage, green pepper, and mushroom and two diet Cokes. The diet Cokes hang somewhat obscenely in a plastic bag. They could be swung, if the shadows solidify and surge.

There's a soft violence of twigs on the snowy ground. I spin and drop the pizza and tighten into a crouch. Some projectile of a thing emerges from the shadows. I freeze.

But it lopes away with the lightness of a being on a smaller, gentler planet.

A dog.

A greyhound.

"Oh my God," the girl behind me yells. What a beautiful animal.

It turns and approaches us with a tentative, curious bounce and a melancholy face. Or, rather, it approaches the pizza.

Transistor Radios in the Other Room

1

Jay Latir came from another time—a time when cartoon bears roamed real woods, selling beer, and Native Americans were called Injuns and served as handy mascots, and elves lived in trees where they baked cookies, and helpful genies and angelic musclemen materialized in kitchens. He came from a time when ads sang and sparkled. His claim to fame was Chuck Wood, a cartoon woodchuck who my illustration instructor pointed out actually more closely resembled a beaver than a woodchuck. Rather than using his teeth to fell trees, Chuck Wood used a Grrrip Saw. The slogan was "Would you buy a Grrrip Saw? Chuck Wood Would." The argument of the ad was: even if you were a magical being and could chew down trees with your teeth, you would still want a Grrrip Saw.

Of course, this drivel was exactly the kind of advertising my classmates and I did NOT want to create.

And yet.

And yet when I told my art school friends I was working for Jay Latir, they were sort of impressed. He had the advertising equivalent of a hit record, no matter how stupid. He had added his little bit to what floated in everyone's head.

So I stepped lightly, with a first-day-of-school nervousness and hope, when I showed up at the small, white, sufficiently contemporary building Jay Latir owned in the suburbs, and met the gracious sil-ver-haired receptionist and made the rounds of people who smiled at me—their smiles not yet sharpened into personalities—from behind IBM Selectrics or inclined drawing boards, and sat at my own draw-ing board and began to squeak magic markers onto paper for money. For a suburban office, this was pretty cool: the main work area had a skylight, and this office development had walking trails and a pond. Leaves were visible through office windows.

The place was actually fun when Jay wasn't around and stiffly fun when he was—as if, when Jay appeared, our feelings dressed up for Sunday. Jay would self-consciously pop into our area—more or less carrying a copy of *Managing by Walking Around* or *The One Minute Manager* or whatever the management book was at the time. He was small boned, bird nosed, and neatly dressed in one of those three-piece suits with tie bars which we all wore in the eighties. He'd speak in a way that was so sincerely fakey you almost felt bad for the guy. It was like Nixon at the family reunion. Jay would aim toward the cluster of us near my drawing board and say, "So how's the new kid doing? The other kids being nice to you? This guy's got it. This guy's the real thing." Awkward shoulder pat. If, say, the keyliner Debbie or the print buyer Amy were leaning over my shoulder, perfumed and jangling with chime-like earrings, giving me grief about some layout, they would, upon seeing Jay, tighten up and reply with coerced nods, and smiles both too broad and too tentative. "Yup. He's doing great." The real affection was conveyed through irony, mock-insults, eye rolls, giving each other shit—I just realized the weirdness of that phrase. The real affection we felt for each other snuck in under the sarcasm we directed at each other.

Keith, the senior art director, would engage Jay and put us out of our misery. Keith had been here five years and he was comfortable enough to let a little boredom drift into his voice. He would say some-thing like, "Don't worry about Big Country here." Keith was one in a line of people who have decided I need a nickname. "We're showing him the ropes."

This allowed Jay to say, "Well, great, then" and amble back to his office.

As soon as Jay left, Keith said, "I rue the day Jay read *Management by Walking Around*. And I'm not much for ruing."

Amy said, "Why couldn't he have read *Management by Skateboarding Around*? That would have been more interesting."

I offered, "*Management by Pogo-Sticking Around*."

Debbie topped that with, "*Management by Walking into Traffic*."

Back in his office, Jay probably heard bubbling laughter and happy squawks, laughter he didn't hear when he was in the room. He wasn't stupid.

2

Of the hundreds of almost random decisions I'd made in that time, one had profound consequences. I thought I'd buy a new car right away, but, cheap and eager to decompress after work, I rode the bus. I enjoyed how the bus snaked through the suburbs, suburbs which you could almost feel becoming a part of the city in the slow slow way such things happen.

I noticed that a pretty girl in a navy-blue preppie anorak/pea coat thing jogged up the steps, smiled and said "Hi" to the bus driver and, still beaming, completing some exchange I didn't hear, sweetly exclaimed, "Hah! I don't think so!" and greeted the people who worked at the Opportunity Workshop, one of whom made a big deal out of shaking her hand. She had short-to-medium brown hair and a small-nosed pretty face and smiling eyes and a scoffing pleasantness to her. Sarcasm balanced her sweetness. It was the holiday season and she had boarded the bus from a stop by a mall, and her voice and face seemed to emerge from the charm and chaos of that time of year, she seemed a gift of the slippery streets and pillow-fight snow storms and urgent, bundled, burdened people and the afternoon darkness and the outbreak of colored lights and candied music. The carols from the mall's speakers brightened as the bus doors sighed open to let Franny in and quieted when they shut.

I wanted very much to meet her, but there wasn't much I could do. Once you're on a bus, you have about as much autonomy as a tree. I noted where she sat that day: about a third of the way back, past the challenged people from the workshop—and positioned myself hopefully on subsequent trips. The first days she sat somewhere else. Three days later, Franny got on the bus, scanned her options in the middle seats, quickly, because nice girls don't want to draw attention to the fact that they are judging people—Don't want to say, in effect, *I will sit next to you and not you.* My competition for her wasn't much: someone who decided that a scowl was simply the best way to meet the world, someone who appeared to be passive-aggressively sleeping, and someone who might actually be complimented if you called him a yuppie. He'd given his expensive briefcase its own seat and was on the verge of giving it a neck massage.

So I won a game no one else was playing.

You're supposed to have a repertoire of snappy opening lines ready for moments like this, and since I am in advertising I should be all about snappy opening lines and strong calls to action, but I always felt foolish even thinking that way, I could never imply "I am charming you now and half an hour from now I will be unwrapping you like a present." I am not that guy. At an art school party, an angry woman painter, who had seen a woman decline to come home with me, had slurred, "You're not the kind of man any woman desires. You are the kind of man some woman will accept. But no woman will ever desire you, so adjust your strategy, you know, accordingly." I thanked her for confirming my deepest fear and she staggered on to enlighten someone else.

So rather than try anything cute—imagine the horror if it had backfired—I just asked Franny if she worked in the mall and then I asked her about what she did and it turned out she was working at a minimalist furniture place over the holiday, that she was in her senior year at the U of M, that she grew up in central Minnesota. She was the daughter of an Italian guy from New York who passed through Alexandria on some GI Bill wanderings, fell in love with the place, fell in love with the local farm girl who would become Franny's mom, and became a farmer's cooperative manager/state senator/real estate investor. When she rose from her seat, she said, "I haven't asked you a thing about yourself."

I said, "Don't worry about it. I'm 'boring white guy 101.'"

She said, "Doubt that," as she exited the bus.

The next night, a bunch of teenage girls who had been shopping at the mall barged onto the bus ahead of Franny. One plopped next to me and immediately turned to talk to her friend in a shocked, conspiratorial voice. Still, I was happy that Franny looked disappointed and shrugged as she waited for the rest of the girls to flow and giggle and whisper through the bus, taking all the seats but a few in the very back, causing briefcase man and the sloucher to cough their disapproval. As soon as the girls left, I looked back, hoping to see Franny but she was talking to an older man—I thought, oh, she doesn't like me, she's just nice to everyone—and saw that the sloucher guy aggressively reasserted his right to angle, limply, across two seats.

As Franny was leaving, she leaned over and said to me, "I think that guy took slouching classes." I said, "It's considered a martial art, in some countries." And then she had to keep moving toward the front of the bus and her stop.

The next day she sat beside me again. Sitting side by side, tilting our heads at an attentive quarter angle, we talked for every ride on the three or four days left in the holiday season. We talked easily. Some of that ease came from feeling like we came from the same world, a world of supper clubs and county fairs and goofy small town newspapers, a world that seemed comic but also somehow nurturing in ways that ran so deep we didn't quite know how to talk about them; in fact, the word "nurturing" would make us both gag, which is why we would just say the name of a hot dish or a local TV show. "Green

Bean Walnut Surprise" and "Casey Jones" and "Pearson's Nut Patties" sounded like trivia, but they were, in fact, spiritual archeology: evidence of a greater luminosity and warmth, evidence of the world where our parents always made us feel safe and prosperous.

We loved the world we invoked, yet we had rejected that world by moving to the Twin Cities. But there was something else, something suggested by where we had met: on a clamoring, chaste, school-evoking bus. It had to do with the Midwestern junior high concept of being "in like" with someone. I was in like with her.

On day four, when the Opportunity Workshop buddy who insisted on always shaking her hand was leaving, he said, maybe to get her attention, which she had directed at me: "Good night, beautiful Elaine Francis Sorrentino."

I ventured, "He's right."

She rebutted, "No," and lowered her eyes.

Then I said, "No, you're beautiful," because I didn't quite know the best thing to say to a woman who is beautiful but doesn't think she's beautiful but hopes she might be viewed by others as beautiful. I didn't know what you say to a woman who looks in a mirror and sees a caricature of herself. Which, as far as I can tell, is pretty much every woman.

Then she looked at me and saw that I was serious when I had said, "No, you're beautiful," and she started to say something else. But then said, "I guess I'm pretty . . . for a linebacker." She had broad shoulders, which she hated.

She continued to look at me, turning as close to full on as she could. What I can only call her soul—the lightest, most agile, most essential part of her—moved and enquired and waited in her eyes, like light in water. She looked vulnerable but also slightly impatient, like she wanted to be argued with, and wanted me to figure that out. Her face—her eyes wide, her mouth just slightly apart—wanted to somehow change and move and respond to me. I almost told her she was beautiful, but then she would have said "no" again. Instead, I said what I felt: "Looking at you is making me a little dizzy."

She considered that, found it pleasing and, I think, surprising, and said, "That's a good thing," somewhat wryly. She turned away from me, with the softness that you turn away from someone after sex. She looked forward and so did I, because the next thing to do on that crowded, cacophonous bus would be to kiss, and the moment demanded not some peck but a kiss which ignites, or at least, surges and suggests, a coupling, and nice kids don't do that on busses.

We both breathed for a few seconds, then she changed the subject, and we were both pleased with how the situation normalized, how we weren't embarrassed or awkward. "So, Twins games on transistor radios in the other room? Do they transport you?"

"That radio was in my room. But, yeah. Totally."

"Oh yeah, of course. You're a boy." Her voice emphasized the word, in a way that brought up all the goofy playground otherness of "girl germs" and "boy germs" and tripping girls to get their attention and girls consulting those origami-like paper oracles that opened like the beaks of baby birds. From what I could tell, the girls asked the paper beaks who their true love was.

3

Because she would not be working after Christmas, we arrived at the day we both knew would be the last day we would ever see each other—unless we made plans to see each other off the bus, unless I said, "I would like to see you." She boarded the bus, sat next to me, and smiled more sheepishly than usual. Neither of us acknowledged what day it was. I asked, "How was your day?" and I could feel my cowardice, my nervousness, and my banality diluting the question into something like an insult. Yet she told me the story of one obnoxious customer who had tried to return a table he had obviously mangled. We talked about our Christmas plans. We almost forgot about what was on my mind and, I suspected, hers. Yes, I was going to Minnisapa and New Luxembourg, to see my sister and brother-in-law. She was going to Alexandria. We talked about that strange feeling when you return home, and suddenly you're not quite your adult self anymore; you're a child or a sibling.

"You don't even need to, like, interact with anyone for it to happen," she said. "It's just walking into the house that does it."

"Yeah, I'm automatically the baby again."

"Oh, God. You so are," said exclaimed, seeing something too loved in me.

"I just want to immediately fall asleep. It's like a drug."

"Me, too. But I also feel this need to help my mom. It's oldest girl stuff. So I'm always, like, tipping over into the pasta. I look totally hot with my head in lasagna."

"I could totally see that." Suddenly distracted, she looked beyond me before I finished what I was saying. Her stop was coming up. She leaned over me to ding the bell but someone else dinged it first.

"Well, I need to go." She looked at me expectantly. Except for a stuttery call to secure a prom date, I'd always been a little buzzed when I started a relationship with a woman. What the drunken art school woman had meant was: no sober woman will ever desire you. I looked up at Franny. I balked: inside me, something swirled and skipped and sabotaged. I chickened out.

The bus pulled up to the stop. I'd waited too long. I thought it would seem rushed and awkward now, with the driver waiting. I just looked at her, like an idiot and said, like it was just another night, "Have a Merry Christmas."

"OK." She said and turned and walked out the door. Even in my panic and self-centeredness, I could see my fear becoming her hurt.

She exited the bus and descended the steps, pointedly looking down, hurrying. I looked out the window as the bus pulled away. I wanted to wave to her. She continued to walk with her head down, she continued to hurry, but she lifted a hand to her eyes.

4

It was January, depressing enough by itself in Minnesota, and I was back at Jay Latir's agency, with my possibilities with Franny gone. I did what I do: I worked.

I soon enough realized that Jay was, in fact, the real thing. That doesn't mean he was hip or cutting edge. Trust me, he wasn't. He was the real thing in that he loved this stuff as much as I did. Like me, he lived to alchemize the blank page. He would brighten when he saw a layout he liked.

Jay had taken me to lunch at some Mexican supper club in the older suburban downtown near the agency. It was so dark in the restaurant you could count the few spikes of sunlight they had not blocked out. The darkness was a kind of good manners, a residue of a cultural memory that nice restaurants are dark. Maracas hung on the wall but then I also noticed poorly lit Carlos Merida lithographs, compositions with the vulnerability of giraffes and the insouciance of certain early '60s jazz. The food was surprisingly substantial and good: the hamburger spiced carefully, the tortillas both browned and steamed, the beans thick, the salsa recently prepared from fresh tomatoes.

As I was doing the ongoing damage control that is eating a burrito in public, Jay said, "Before I moved to Minnesota, I went to law school for a year but then took a job in an advertising agency in New York to make ends meet during the day and I realized that law is this great structure built out of fear and worry, that it is all about what could go wrong and how can people disappoint you or how bad can we be without getting caught, and I realized I didn't want to do that, and then in the day, at the advertising agency, I had so much fun, and I realized that advertising celebrated life." He meant every word of this.

The problem was, Jay loved advertising but he just wasn't good enough, at least not any more. Jay was a hack and hackdom might be a natural state, but it might also be something that happens to you but that happens invisibly and obliquely, like a disease: your work falls in a rut and then you take a natural possessive pride in this not-quite-good work and your work gets even blander and things that might inspire or provoke you start to feel wrong, so you fall even deeper into your rut. Jay fell into the same word play every time he started an assignment. For any product that was in any way customized he would always say, "What sets us apart is how we put it together." The first time you hear that, you like the play of "apart" and "together." The seventh time you hear it, you cringe.

Don't ask me how I know this—a humble pause after a bad idea, a look of soft, private appreciation when he saw an idea he never would have thought of—but I think Jay was smart enough to know the truth about himself and his little suburban agency. I started interviewing.

I took long weekends and faux sick days preceded by hours of stagey sniffling and coughing. I worked with the new writer, the maliciously named Brian O'Brien, a chunky Irish-Catholic guy who had transformed his boyhood habit of mumbling ironically in the direction of clergy into a marketable skill. We created punning, snarky ads with big headlines and simple visuals. We searched funny archival photos and made them into ads for local bookstores and bowling alleys and donut shops. We thought what we were doing was ground-breaking, although even at these few years' distance what strikes me is its sameness and smugness.

I didn't get hired. I did get sloppy, not in my work for Jay (which was actually getting better) but in my habits.

Jay found a layout on my drawing board while I was out with the gang for lunch.

We came back in, laughing about some joke I've long since forgotten. Jay was standing, scowling, at my station.

"Einwald, did you do this?" He held up an ad that said, "When Henry VIII needed some time away from the wives, he went bowling."

"Yes," I said sheepishly.

Everyone disappeared into their work stations and lowered their heads.

"On my time?"

"Yes," I said.

"Have you done this before?"

"Yes," I said.

"Then get the hell out of here," he said, and shattered the board over his knee.

I erased myself. Flustered as I was, it was chastening how little time it took: I packed up my few personal things, my markers, my pencils, a few sketch pads I used for concepting, and a few posters. While removing a Blue Note records poster I'd had since art school, I ripped the corner off. I stood and cringed for a minute at the fragment, which separated the name Eric Dolphy and the letters "unch!" from "Out To Lunch!" from the rest of the poster. Then I yelled "son of a bitch" and reduced the poster to shreds

Ann and Keith and Debby stood a respectful distance from me and said reassuring and kind things and hugged me and shook my hand. Brian, who had written the headline, did not leave his office, and I didn't look at him when I passed. And then I left that hopeful sunlit office forever, waiting fifteen horrible minutes for the bus, and returned to my apartment; the apartment was a post-war box but my post-war box, neat and well furnished with poster-sized, foam-core-mounted stats of Garamond letter forms, their serifs delicate wings.

The apartment felt tender and tentative. My mother was still alive then but I couldn't bear to call her.

EMILY

The Waves capsized me.

More specifically, the reaction of one Todd Guernica, a suburban Seattle punk, to the Virginia Woolf experimental stream of consciousness novel, *The Waves*, capsized me. He was gorgeous, in a lanky sinewy yet dimpled kind of way; a mountain biker and skateboarder, he had the confidence that elides into the cruelty of certain jocks. He was vaguely socialist, but that seemed just another way to get laid. And he really really didn't like *The Waves*. He hated it, assiduously.

I was teaching *The Waves* because it was the opposite of a romance novel. I never understood the appeal of such books, of either the low or high variety. I disdained their heat.

The whole point of literature is coolness, isn't it? And not in that "that's really keen" sense of coolness that the modern usage has degenerated into, not in the "cool jeans!" "cool haircut," "cool lunchbox!" "cool shoelaces!" sense but in the "elegant disinterested subtleties of the mind" sense of coolness. The whole point of literature is the respite it gives you from the sweat on the brow, the electricity on the skin, the flutter in the gut, the inflammation in the crotch—all that goddamn hopeful, hopeless rubbing. The beauty of *The Waves* was that there was no soap opera, just six monologues, six chilled bonfires of consciousness and character. My fellow teachers had warned me against teaching it.

"Mr Guernica, what did you think of *The Waves?*"

"I thought it sucked."

A twitter of laughter. I should have stopped the exchange there.

But I insisted on engaging with him. "*The Waves* is experimental. What kind of experiment is Virginia Woolf conducting here?"

"How to make upper class twits even more unlikeable?" He'd had his moment. He was tired of this exchange.

"What do you mean by unlikeable?"

Nothing.

"What do you mean by unlikeable?"

"I mean I want to punch Bernard with his 'phrases' and Louis with his faggy whatever in the fucking face."

The class roared with laughter, a many-fanged beast. I reddened. "You can't speak like that."

"I mean, seriously dude," he continued, having an imaginary conversation with Bernard or Louis.

"Shut up," I said, not as emphatically as I'd intended, not emphatically enough to stop him.

He was still addressing Louis or Bernard, the effete narrators. "Work as a busboy for ten minutes and see how much you're still whining about your life at Oxford."

I grabbed his desk, leaned into his face and yelled, "I told you to shut up." A spray of my spit hit him.

"I was making a point," he said. "I thought this was a discussion."

"Get out of my classroom," I said.

He'd just wanted to give the other kids a story about his awesomeness. "That time in AP English when Guernica said *The Waves* sucked."

He was realizing what he had done.

I was realizing the choices I've made: if only I hadn't taught *The Waves*, if only I hadn't insisted on my weird arctic interpretation of literature, if only I hadn't called on Todd, if only I had cut him off earlier, if only I hadn't spat at a student. The subjunctives evaporated: I had, I had, I had, I had, I had. The room was filled with beings and objects who hadn't destroyed their career.

I could see the adult man, better than a lot of adult men, who would regret this.

He said, "I'm sorry!" and left the room. I was given a one week leave of absence.

PORTER

I know the boyish light of baseball. I have walked in the fog of a June morning down the dirt road to a ball field in Marais de Peine, Wisconsin—on the Mississippi river, just across from Minnisapa, Minnesota. I hit the ball into the mist and retrieved it until the rest of the boys came and I stayed through the sweet light of morning and the thirsty light of afternoon and the shadowed light of dusk and the bruised light of sunset.

At lunch time, when the other boys went home, I counted the money I had stolen from my passed-out mother that morning. I had crept into her room. I would often see a man lying, naked, near her. I would glimpse his sex, smug and glistening as a rat, lolling in the sheets.

My mother did not always walk the earth in shame and fury. My mother had been in the car with my father when they were struck, head-on. She said the eyes heading toward them yearned for a collision. My father was killed. My mother bore marks across her face which men ignored only when they were very drunk. And something else happened: it was as if her cells were milk which had gone bad.

In Snotty's bar, kinder men than the men in my mother's bed told me how my father would take me here before he died. I felt the happiness we call home as I approached the bar: The way the screen door would welcome me with its promised flicker of jukebox lights, its sounds of voices and pinball and country music, its malty smells. When you opened it, the door would sigh in the way that certain screen doors sigh. Snotty, would say, "The usual?" and open a Grape Nehi for me and grab a bag of Lay's potato chips. I would sometimes be given a sandwich which the bartender supposedly "couldn't finish." If I spun on my bar stool, I would see sunlight slant through the window and awaken the smoky air. This is what I know of light.

Wispy Banal Demons

1

Thursday is a good day by my standards but not, probably, by yours.
I wake at 9:00 to cottony light and the patient mess of my living
room and the sound of my alarm clock losing its cartoon mind at
the other end of my apartment. I've needed that alarm clock more,
not less, these days of not working. Without it, I might spend the
day in a decathlon of half-consciousness and inertia. I might sample
sleep, half-sleep, boredom, naps, sluggish three-quarter wakefulness,
and a sadness that feels like exhaustion and an exhaustion that feels
like fear. I might lie there while snowplows scraped and thudded in
the alley behind me and I watched fifty-seven percent of the episode
of Bugs Bunny and His Friends where Sylvester the Cat joins Birds
Anonymous because he has a "two bird a day habit."
Instead, today, the alarm fetches me down the hall to the bedroom
and from there—upright, chilly, in my underwear, able to actually
feel the chaos of my unwashed hair (which has apparently made me
even less aerodynamic than usual)—I might as well get started on the
day. I squirm into a robe. I make coffee in the almost sacramental way
that those of us who cringe with recognition at being called "yuppies"
make coffee. I make coffee in the way that Franny and I made coffee
for each other. I pour filtered water into the coffee maker, tap out yesterday's muddy grounds, measure the whole beans I have purchased

from the nearby specialty shop, whir the grinder, breathe the now fragrant air and tip the dry coffee into the clean filter. It falls in the soothing way that grain pours. I close the lid and press the button: the brewing process begins.

But although I will follow the same steps, this is nothing like that, this has nothing to do with that almost overwhelming tenderness of those first mornings when you realize that you really want to be with each other. We would bring in the cream-lightened coffee and shining fruit braids on lovely white trays with blonde wood handles. Coffee was an extension of sex, it was afterplay: it smelled nice; it made us happy; it said, *I don't regret this, I will not skulk away.* But she has now skulked away, quite emphatically.

Now in the morning light I also miss the coffee that the grown-ups drank when I was a kid, the mockable coffee of mockable farm towns, which came from big cheap cans of Folgers and goofy percolators with obscure inner workings. The brewing coffee danced in that little glass do-hickey on top of the percolator; my mom served the coffee in pink acrylic cups that looked exactly like what Betty Rubble would serve coffee in.

As the warm yuppie coffee I now evidently prefer drips into the beaker, I look at the phone. What might it possibly connect to? No partners, no soul mates, no parents.

Now, I feel hungover, obscurely poisoned by my experience at the factory, the bad life decisions which led me here, my dishonest treatment of my supervisor, the fact that the other kids didn't play with me on the first day of school, or just the Terry Gilliam industrial video *feng shui* of the place—the faintly metallic air, all those grays and greens. I also feel weirdly depressed that I wouldn't be going back there. I kinda missed Banjo Boy and Eunice. I missed the camaraderie of break rooms, even though I'd screwed that up, and the well-wishing of people in parking lots. I missed how I made things better by sorting out the bad mugs and letting the good ones go out into the world.

Instead, here I was doing no work, making absolutely nothing better, communing with the wispy banal demons of my own thoughts, the thoughts that percolate when I have too much time, too little human contact, too little purpose. It's a good thing I have an appointment with Sargent Serenity because otherwise all I could look forward to today was the subtle but yucky intensification of my own character defects: Annoyance torquing into rage, regret thickening into paralysis, wistfulness frothing into self-pity.

I realize that I will be late if I don't get a move on.

2

Sargent Serenity has an idiosyncratic approach to therapy that includes half hour appointments. The idea is that errands heal us, that errands are brisk and rinsing. Serenity is legitimately but obscurely licensed—he can charge money to hear intimacies and calm me down, but I'm not sure what exactly he is. Psychologist, for sure. But he is an impressively educated former Marine, former Jesuit who thinks very highly of William James' *The Varieties of Religious Experience* and Marcus Aurelius *Meditations*, of all things.

His office is about a half mile away, next to a diner, a laundromat, and a place that sells supplies for making your own beer. Grand Avenue—it's a bracelet of small industrious dreams.

I walk. Per Serenity's instructions, I notice with a little more vigor than usual but it seems to defeat the point of a walk to turn it into an assignment. But, still, I look and see:

- the bare branches of many trees, without nests;
- a sort of Hasidic beard of leaves, high in the bare branches of a tree, oh yes, it is a nest;
- the not-quite-bare branches of a few trees, with a few disoriented brown leaves, fidgeting in the wind;
- the sun in the middle of the milky gray sky.

When I first notice it, the sun feels as soft as the moon. But as I direct my gaze at its glow, I flinch from its insistence. Then, as I walk, my eyes recovering, I notice the glory of creation, as Serenity commanded: a dog, sheepishly squatting and straining out a little nautilus of poop; his pretty shock-haired owner, holding the leash with one hand and fishing for a bag with the other; the dog starting after a squirrel (that crazy squirrel: a puff of fur that darts as jerkily as a flip book); a woman in a harried car, a decaying AMC Gremlin, which twitches back and forth in a parking space as traffic flows by. She is parking by the Bibelot, a stylishly hippie-ish gift shop, perhaps to find something beautiful.

I ascend the stairs, which feel like the stairs to a detective agency— they have a dry, defeated, but rich smell—and am once again surprised by the name Tim Griffin on the door, because we always call him Sergeant Serenity or some variation thereof. He has a huge office so he can do group therapy, with the crappiest furniture ever to adorn a serious office: aggressively plastic orange chairs that look like they were stolen from my senior high lunch room, a metal desk so charmless it appears to be in storage even when it isn't, and weird quasi-woodcuts of what are either tractors or pterodactyls. That said, the light in the place is wonderful. He's on the second story, with a parking lot behind him, and the skim-milk light streams in these big, multi-paned windows.

I'm a little nervous as I climb the stairs, because I'm not sure he's going to like my report from my field trip.

Please understand: I mock Serenity, but I like Serenity. We all do. He listens like someone who gets paid to listen. He puts up with our soliloquies and nudges us toward health. To wit: Death hurts but happens to everyone; my breakup and my job loss were the result of correctable flaws in how I approach the world and those flaws are tied to deep patterns, so I need to be patient. We talk about numbness— like pain, numbness has its uses—and honesty—he's increasing the dosage—and forgiveness.

But Serenity also talks about things the garden-variety counselor doesn't talk about: the need to "meet the secret demands of the universe." That is his definition of spirituality, I think from William James. I suspect that there was a moment in Vietnam when Serenity saw something that made him think that he could no longer look away from those demands, a moment when he had to choose between becoming spiritual or becoming crazy. Serenity has clearly rented a room in the abyss.

This experience has made Serenity both rigorous, in his sense of what is at stake, and forgiving, in his understanding that progress and stumbling are often the same thing. If Serenity fails at what he does, people sometimes put guns in their mouths and spray walls with the inert residue of their being. Until it was recently expanded, my idea of failure was losing the Cheese Whiz account.

It is Serenity's forgiveness that I step toward, that brightens my mood when I knock on the clouded-glass window in his door. When you are in his office, you have permission to be completely self-centered, to essentially vomit whatever rant or confusion is in your head. That's the theory, at least.

Unfortunately, Serenity does have his tells. The man has expressive knees and he sits open-legged in his orange tear drop chair and starts to bounce them like basketballs being dribbled when you're going on about something inane.

The knees bounce pretty hard as I go on about my time at the factory. Serenity actually looks like a Tim Griffin. Or maybe a Chuck or Jim. He looks military: tall, lean, thin-featured, sandy-haired, small-eyed and fierce-eyed, more efficient than graceful. He wears khakis and shirts whose colors are variations on mud. He moves with a slightly coiled, strategic quality which makes him seem ready for a fight. He has the uneasiness of a man who just quit smoking. He quit ten years ago.

"So how was your time at the factory?"

"I don't know. It was weird."

"That doesn't tell me a lot."

"'Weird' is the best I can do right now."

"Will you be going back there?"

"No," I said.

Serenity frowned.

"Something weird happened. They offered me a job."

"OK."

"You didn't anticipate that?" I asked.

"I wanted you to get out into the world. That means everything won't turn out predictably. How did you respond to the job offer?"

"I said, 'no.'"

"Interesting. I'd ask you this: is someone who can afford to turn down a job offer truly unlucky?"

"I know. I'm an ungrateful jerk."

"It was a real question—not a way to make you feel bad."

There is a sigh and a bump outside the door, an ascending thumping and scritching and chaos, a command in a voice I almost recognized, an explanation in a voice I now recognized, and a whimper in what I knew was a dog's voice, a sad attempt to make inflection do what only language can. Serenity and I exchange a concerned eyebrow flex and he heads toward the door. I follow. Two shadows move on the other side of the milky glass: a bald man whose beard suggests something one part Old Testament and one part skid row, yet he moves with a former second baseman's quickness, suited to lateral motion and quick scoops—Porter, I realize. Behind Porter is a long-snouted dog with ears perked up like the flaps of the flying nun's hat.

Porter smiles with relief, almost crying, when he sees us.

3

The human beings look at each other and the dog. The dog—
a fawn-colored girl with a white tuxedo patch—arrows toward me
and leans against my hip so hard that, if I were to move, she would fall
over. I pet her; I don't think I've ever encountered a creature so guile-
less. If you put your face on my hip, I'd probably pet you. When she
shivers, I hug her. I immediately know why Porter had this dog and
why he had kept this dog. I hadn't touched another being in months.

Serenity says, "So who do we have here?"

Porter says, "I don't know her name. I've been calling her Honey."

She doesn't respond to the name.

She suddenly twists away from me and begins to inspect the
room. She alights and sniffs and decides.

"Is she housebroken?"

"I'm pretty sure. We spent the night in my car. And she whined
and wagged her nose at the door so I let her out."

Serenity asks, "So what's going on here, Porter? Where did you
get this dog?"

While he waits for his answer, Serenity doesn't keep the dog from
inspecting his office. She isn't any more impressed with it than the
rest of us are. She plunges her nose into Serenity's wastebasket. Turns
out he has a jones for Almond Joy bars.

I say, "Sometimes you feel like a nut."

Serenity glares at me.

When Honey dips her long muzzle into the wastebasket again and pulls another Almond Joy, Porter, who usually speaks like the King James Bible, says, "Oh Honey bunny don't."

Serenity says to Porter. "I'm glad that you're trying to do the right thing by this animal."

Porter breaks down. "I mean, I love her. She's so beautiful. But I can't take care of her. I was afraid to sleep last night. She shivered and whined and I didn't know what to do until I found an old blanket in the back of my car and wrapped her in it. I could tell she didn't like the cold. She almost spasmed when . . . so I kept my car running all night. And then when I left to use the bathroom, she went all crazy."

Serenity says, "So," and then inserts a therapist's pause, "what do you want to do next, Porter? What's the next right thing?"

Porter sighs. "Call the humane society."

Serenity nods. "There's a yellow pages in my desk drawer. You can use my phone."

Honey leans against my leg. I become her advocate. "Has she been fed? Has she had water?"

"I got some bread sticks and pepperoni and fed her that." And then he says, in the voice of someone who wears shame like a backpack, "But I didn't think about water."

Serenity says to me, "You can use the bathroom down the hall." He hands me the key, which is on a large Mickey Mouse doll. "And I think I've got something that might work as a bowl." He pulls a chocolate Cool Whip container from his desk and dumps some crayons onto the desk.

I take her down the hall with me. I'd never known an animal so trusting. She laps up the water. She'd been thirsty.

When we return, Porter leans over her and hugs her. The dog endures his love sweetly. "We found your family, Honey. It's gonna be okay. Everything's gonna be okay." Tears moisten Porter's face and then more tears run over the moistness. Honey squirms but does not leave his grasp. When her people arrive, they are overjoyed. She knows them: she points and scrunches and then runs toward them and circles them. Her name is Caper. Saving a dog named Caper transforms grocery shopping and sitcoms which, in four words, was the rest of my day. Thanks to my friend Porter, this would be the day I met a dog named Caper.

EMILY

You'll have to excuse me; you'll have to excuse the hysteria which is swarming around my nerve ends and the parenthetical overdrive which is my mind at the moment; you'll have to excuse me as I lie on my back with a stranger above me putting awful things into my mouth. Metallic things, rubbery things, cottony things which are bloody when removed, scraping things, needles, monsoons of salt and grit, body parts. (Well, fingers.) Insistent, whining, high-pitched things. My teeth become mist and the mist floats into my vision and sparkles. I wonder if I should call someone's attention to this. I am trying to ignore the millimeters that separate me from bloody catastrophe, I am trying to ignore my paralyzed cheek and my unladylike drool. I am trying to forget the metal mantis that just inoculated my gums. I am staring dizzily at the ceiling. I am trying to transcend. I don't normally do transcend.

The chattery relentless layering of my mind has transformed this dentist's chair into the scene of other traumas induced by other moments of helplessness—most recently drunken and complicit and, before that, innocent or at least apparently innocent if the prevailing good press about five-year-old girls is to be believed. With the weight of these traumas pressing down on me, I am having trouble breathing.

PORTER

She would flip my hand with her nose when she wanted to be petted.
When she shivered, she would lean on me. She would headbutt me
gently after I fed her breadsticks and pepperoni. She would harumph
when she finally got comfortable in my back seat.

I will not know the peace of the chin nuzzle, the head scritch, the
butt pat.

Saint Francis was the greatest saint because he knew the broadest
love.

Filling the Jar

1

After Jay Latir fired me, I entered a preview of my present purgatory: reluctantly applying for unemployment, spending too much time in my underwear, filling my days with sour introspection. I was lucky or perhaps not. I got a job again in three weeks, at a big bright boring byzantine agency downtown that evidently did every cereal commercial ever made and may or may not have known the whereabouts of the Pillsbury dough boy. (There are twelve of them, in secret locations.) Every morning, I entered the Minneapolis skyline which, I have since heard, contains only buildings which resemble wheat or water. I boarded a brisk commuter bus that was invigorating without being cheerful. My fellow riders were reluctantly awake people in Burberry coats and navy blue business dresses and tennis shoes. (They held their work shoes.) I strode through big automatic glass doors and ascended in an elevator that, for a moment, made me feel as weightless as a thought.

I accumulated a paragraph on my resume: I kept my head down and did a few pretty good TV spots for a lawn mower client, then a few really good TV spots for an insecticide company and a bunch of okay but highly visible ads for a big cereal company. Eventually, I started doing some more daring freelance for restaurants and video rental stores with Brian O'Brien from Latir and Associates, who had joined me at Mega Meta and Maxi a few months after I had been fired by Jay Latir. They were print ads, with the lovely discipline of print ads—no editor or music or special effects to save a bad idea, just you and a writer and an expectant rectangle of blank paper. Brian found an account executive who could handle the parts of the business that required a suit, tie, and rudimentary social skills, and we opened O'Brien Einwald Davis.

We rented office space in the top floor of a formerly vacant hotel in the part of downtown which had been as forlorn and modest as a bum's fedora but which now was being branded as the warehouse district. As we stepped off the elevator on the first day of business, after having breakfast at the vaguely alt diner across the street where the black lipsticked waitresses were ritualistically rude to us, the sunlight streamed in like a reference letter from God, and we could see Brian and Scott's desks and then my drawing board in our vast hopeful brick-lined loft and then, as I walked to my drawing board, I saw the spouts and vents and hatchways and tar paper and sooty bricks of the ceilings of the other buildings on our block and then above that, spectacularly, triumphantly, excessively blue sky. Brian joked, "I'm going to go name the plants," and it took me a little bit to get the joke, because Brian is given to obscure biblical and theological quips, but he was right: the first day at a new agency is as close to feeling like Adam in the Garden of Eden as any of us will ever get. As I looked out on the scribbly infrastructure of roofs, even the fear in my gut was buoyant.

2

The fear I felt that first day soon seemed unfounded. O'Brien Einwald and Davis thrived. We won accounts. We hired people. Business was so good I was almost glad I wasn't in a relationship. Almost.

Toward the end of our first year, I was having lunch downtown with Pooch Labrador from Minnisapa when Franny materialized, oblivious to me, walking briskly past on the sidewalk outside.

I said to Pooch. "Someone I haven't seen in years just walked past. I have to catch her."

Pooch said, "Sure, abandon your Minnisapa friends."

I was up from the table and didn't exchange his banter. It was fall, and I ran out without even my sport coat. The probability of rejection gathered inside me, but I tried to move so fast that I didn't notice it. I pushed the weight of the door open and emerged into the chilled air. She was halfway down the block. I sprinted toward her.

"Hey, Franny!"

It was my turn to risk getting hurt.

She turned and, when she saw me running after her, smiled.

"Hey!"

"How ya been? It's been ages."

"Great. I'm working for a non-profit that gets help from this law firm."

"Cool. I'm working at an agency downtown. Actually, I'm kind of a partner in one." I regretted bragging. I was breathing slightly harder than I wanted to be.

Over the months since we last spoke, I'd formulated an anti-strategy, a headlong commitment to the moment when I might see her again: I would not hesitate, I would say what was in my heart, and I would accept whatever pain was coming. I was tired of rejecting myself.

"I regret that we didn't stay in touch at all." 'Stay in touch' was lame. Her face softened and, perhaps, forgave me.

"Me too," she said.

So I said, "Do you want to get together sometime?" I knew this was woefully vague; it didn't give her an easy out.

"I've got plans this Saturday night but how about next Saturday?"

We had dinner at a restaurant called Table of Contents and it would become our place, and our connection was as inevitable this time as it was awkward the first time. That may be why the thing I want most now, now that she has left forever, is to sit at a window table at Table of Contents, which was both our favorite restaurant and a part of a bookstore, in the European softness of prosperous St Paul, watching the occasional pedestrian walk past with the fizz of esteem you get when you are about to enter a bookstore. I want to be trying some menu item whose ingredients I will always want to remember but always forget—fennel? tarragon? saffron? —and making some smart remark to Franny along the lines of: "Basically, Europeans discovered the rest of the world, crossed unbelievably scary oceans, because they were trying to find some decent take out . . . " and Franny would say something like, "I wonder if the men on the ships got to eat anything made with the spices." She would say it in a way that I would feel not corrected, but completed; the humane notes of her conversation, sliding under my jazzy dithering, my cartoony second-rate ad guy mind. We started kissing before we even got back to the couch in her apartment. All those days on the bus and all those months when we thought we would never connect had counted as foreplay, at least to me.

Within two months, we were living together. I remember those months as a golden age. She moved into my place in a Victorian on Summit Avenue, once home of the railroad rich, now subdivided into condos for the merely affluent. Our home felt like a refuge from the frustrations of our long days in the world—mine spent building a business, hers spent fighting for the innocent and oppressed. We came home happily exhausted, with the frustrations of people who think they are fighting the good fight, whether that means, and talked about our days over dinner, sometimes frozen entrees, just as often take out—spicy mustard chicken and Vietnamese egg rolls with their iridescent noodle fillings from the Lotus; crab cakes and southern fried chicken from Dixies. We fell into the couch for *Seinfeld* or *Mad About You*, easing into each other. Pooch Labrador had said, "Put a penny into a jar every time you have sex during the first year you're together and take one out every time after that and you won't empty the jar." We were filling the jar.

In the mornings, there were expensive coffees ground and brewed in our kitchen and thickened with cream; on weekends, there were croissants from Café Con Amore.

She softened my aesthetic—which has been described as "Dave Brubeck opens a sports bar"—without eliminating it, adding fabrics and distressed antiques and oxidized metals. Thanks to her, we lived a soundtracked life; she introduced me to brooding, shapely, almost-country music: the Cowboy Junkies' *Caution Horses*, Los Lobo's *Kiko*, The Jayhawks *Hollywood Town Hall*, REM's *Automatic for the People*. There were suddenly twice as many friends, mine added to hers.

They weren't vacations—we were too busy for that—but there were weekends in Montreal, San Francisco, and Chicago. Montreal was sadder than we expected (she observed that the money had left in the '70s); San Francisco was harsher ("everyone is either driving a Mercedes or sleeping under one"); Chicago, where she'd been a poor intern helping even poorer people, was our surprising favorite. It hadn't changed. We just had money now.

The cities we visited had their sadnesses but they couldn't over-come our happiness—as we walked their streets canyoned with skyscrapers and enjoyed their sidewalk cafes and museums and their theaters and their parks. Love transformed consumption into conver-sation.

We fought occasionally, but our fights were tactical and situa-tional. Times we were both too tired; times when we'd insufficiently negotiated the details of living together—me, arriving late for meals she had planned; me, leaving something unattended to; and, less frequently, her, not expressing some assumption or expectation. We thought these fights were healthy and they probably were. Something else destroyed us.

I can't talk about this without sounding like a dope or a yuppie. Takeout food, good alt music, weekend jaunts. It shouldn't quite add up to a life. But the world was softer when she was around. The world was smarter when she was around.

EMILY

One week after my scene with Todd Guernica, my leave of absence concluded, I stood outside the school and felt the incisive gleam of the many glass doors, the perfumed sweaters of the girls, the foreign effervescence of their tangled voices, the Stonehenge of boys' bodies and the factory of their talk and the swarm and stink of the exhaust of a dozen busses and the unreachable normalcy in a colleague's voice as she asked, repeatedly, "Are you all right?"

"No."

PORTER

The last time I saw my Mother, she was in a chair in a nursing home.

"Mom, do you know who I am?"

"You're a son-of-a-bitch!"

"Mom, do you know who I am?"

"You're just going to lie to me, you motherfucker!"

"Mom, do you know who I am?"

"Take a goddamn hint and leave!"

"Mom."

"I don't want that," she says, and knocks a glass of water off the bed stand. I grab a towel from her bathroom and wipe it up and wring out the towel in the sink.

"Mom, it's Mother's Day. There are flowers here for you. I'm setting them here."

I set them down. "I love you," I say.

I leave.

I hear her say, loudly, to no one, as I step into the nursing home hall, "What?"

There is, in her voice, above the malice and metal, a softening, a flicker of confusion and recognition. I am tempted to re-enter the room, but I do not.

Disillusioned Chartreuse

1

It would be inaccurate to say I have nothing to do Friday. My autonomic nervous system is being its usual go-getter self. My metabolism reports for duty. The weather, or the second law of thermodynamics, might churn up something.

I am supposed to have lunch with Pooch Labrador. I've liked Pooch since I met him when I moved to Minnisapa. On first impression, the Minnisapa guys merge into a single wise-cracking, clean-cut mass. But I noticed soon enough that Pooch didn't call me by a different nickname every week. (The rest of them did.) While what everyone noted about Pooch was his intelligence—a skipped grade, effortlessly at the top of his class, A-pluses on physics exams he'd forgotten to study for—his ambition was the opposite of everyone else's. Most people are ordinary and work their whole life to be seen as extraordinary. He was extraordinary and worked his whole life to be seen as ordinary—a highly successful, idealized version of ordinary but still. He'd gone from business school to a product manager gig at a software company and then to a CFO position at a competing agency. He loved the business dinner, the golf outing, the time spent around people like me—the creatives who wrote the headlines and designed the ads.

The phone rings. It's Pooch.

"Yes, Duane, how you doing," he says. I wince. I'm in one of those pockets of life where the phrase "How you doing?" poses difficulties.

"You know, can't complain," I say. This isn't exactly a lie.

"Oh, good," Pooch says with the soft distraction of a man getting to something less pleasant. "Unfortunately, I can't make lunch today. Our books are being reviewed by a big potential client and I've got to divest us of some strip joints."

I don't say anything for a few moments, because I don't know what to say. My conversational incompetence suggests that maybe I never had any business being a partner in an agency.

He then says, "Sorry. I've got to pull numbers together this weekend," to emphasize that he really is busy. He knows that, for me, a canceled lunch empties the day. Of course, Pooch lives in a world, where it is almost expected that you will reschedule a lunch at least once, that this is a sign of one's vitality, of one's brimming to-do list, of one's indispensability.

"Don't worry about it," I say, and saying that shouldn't require bravado but it does. "I'll call you next week and we'll reschedule."

"Good," he says, with the cheery briskness of a happy person conducting business.

"Have a good one."

I probably won't.

2

A quantity of minutes passes. As I lean against the back of my futon couch, and stare at the silent TV, I feel the usual wispy abyss gathering around me. The air judges me, my thoughts touch me like air, I become queasy; my soul puddles; and this miasma of room-and-self suggests that I am fundamentally damaged. I am bullied by ephemera.

The canceled lunch reminds me of my canceled life. I envy the conventionally unemployed who are free to seek the next 9-to-5 soul-destroying trudge. I am contractually obligated to not get a job and, yet, my funds drain away, my talent atrophies, and my reputation fades. And I have to sit here, on my futon, and take it—take it and be grateful. I have clothes. I have food. I have shelter. And yet something is going bad. I know I have a soul because that's precisely where something is going bad. A visitor to my apartment would see nothing amiss.

The smallest pilot light of health in my brain says: do not let this play out. Do not let the day do its dirty business on you.

So I walk, per Serenity's instructions.

So I walk, because it is as close as I can get to breaking up with myself. My petty, ungrateful, lazy, venomous, hissing and ranting self. But the sky is dismal-colored—as gauzy yet dingy as a tarp. The sky may be chartreuse but that is such an odd color for a sky I can't quite believe it. Disillusioned chartreuse. Somewhere between light filtering through a Coke bottle and light filtering through a canvas. It is one of those colors so subtle it makes me suspect I am alone in the universe.

I keep thinking that I had somehow botched the simple exchange I'd just had with Pooch, that I had somehow injected it with triviality and neuroses and cluelessness. I can't point to any words that I regretted, yet my sense of the conversation is that I had revealed some fundamental, invisible-to-me weakness and weirdness.

I circle the block and walk south of Grand, into the neighborhoods filled with the homes of attorneys and tenured professors, the kind of house Franny and I were shopping for before the breakup: solid without being oppressive, prosperous without being showy, with patriarchal woodwork and generous windows. But the big craftsmen and Victorians are empty, their occupants at law firms or universities, the sidewalks responsibly shoveled but slick with the mist.

One walk isn't shoveled. Steps are embossed into the snow. Someone isn't quite holding it together.

My feet mash white snow into silver sludge and I return to my apartment.

That afternoon, the room continues to sour. I strain to find something that might fill the day.

EMILY

I am staring at the poorly drawn tree on the ceiling, with its fingery branches and smeary daubs of either blossoms or birds. I am gripping myself like a straightjacket. I am trying to tell myself what my therapist, less a Freudian than a Seussian, tells me: that this is not that. Of course, he hadn't considered that this may be more awful than that, objectively considered. There were not needles involved with that; there was not scraping. That didn't take so damn long, what with men being men.

There is a slight problem, though. Just the slightest of problems which I may feel compelled to draw attention to.

The room is filling with water.

I close my lungs against the murderous trickle. Deft marine creatures hover above me in masks and poke and scrape at me; I try not to disturb the joking marine creatures, who do not have a word for "drowning." They don't know how strange they are, with their mermaid twinkle and walrus smugness. My heart accelerates; random tendons seek the power of speech, like that first fish who improvised a lung.

I surge out of my chair. My legs wobble, consciousness abandons me like a disgusted friend, and while I start to protest, I crash to what I presume will be the floor.

PORTER

This is what I will be, for the rest of my days: I will be the man who walks the streets, carrying treats for your dog, feeling the absence of love in my hands and arms like a small terrible breeze. I will be the man who brightens a little too much at your dog's love.

Aubergine Piggy Banks

1

The phone rings. It is Emily. She is at her dentist; she's had a fainting spell and needs a ride to an emergency room in a hospital down the hill from Grand Avenue.

The day clarifies into a series of actions: hanging up the phone, putting on my coat and my boots and my one glove, using the rag-rug from my mom's house to sop up the delicate puddle my boots had made, walking to the car, and starting the engine. I still have a BMW, after all; I still have the benediction of a brand, which I now think of only when giving someone else a ride. I turn onto a side street and then onto Grand Avenue and Snelling and then 94 and 280 with the happy diligence of a dog finally given a task. I arrive in another St Paul neighborhood which, like Grand Avenue, has the softness and charm of a village.

When I enter the dentist's office, a bell chimes, announcing me. The smocked staff smiles behind the desk, and when I say "Emily?" they point into the waiting room, locating her between the aquarium and two people waiting for their appointments. The people waiting for their appointments stare into the air in front of them, determined not to acknowledge their surroundings. Emily is sitting, talking, with a dental assistant. Even though a towel blossoms on her face, covering her vigorous eyes and elegant nose, and her skin is glazed with sweat, and her short hair is mussed, she still has somehow retained the quality of her beauty which makes her seem like she comes from multi-generational money, even though she doesn't. Her eyes catch mine and apologize. I nod back. The orange and blue fish in the aquarium dart in my peripheral vision. I've read somewhere that fish are only conscious of the most recent moment in their lives: they appear to think but what they do is awaken again and again. There is an anxious, clinical feeling to the air, the low hum and remembered mist of dentistry, a foreboding that these brightnesses and smiles and clip-art struggle to soften.

Emily points at her damaged face and says through the towel, "I'm an idiot."

I say "bummer." A part of me darts; trapped in this strange place. I try to judge how I can best help her, what will be enough to steady her but not too intimate. The most baffling thing: even though she's God's gift to blue jeans, I don't have feelings toward her. It's as if my feelings always wear some sort of prophylactic when I'm around her. Well, not that baffling. She's the kind of girl who's been reminding boys like me that she likes them as friends since she was thirteen.

As if to emphasize this she says, "I was going to call Porter, but I don't think he's a fan of blood."

"That was kind of you," I say.

"He's a good guy," she shrugs.

"Okay. I don't want to get all handsy on you, so what should I do?" A better man would know what to do. Prince Charming didn't ask the Princess what the procedure was here.

She lifts the towel. Her nose is bloody; the skin around it, purpling.

"I'm fine. Just spot me."

She wobbles up and then steps forward, tentatively.

"Like riding a bike." She says, through the towel which she has reapplied.

"Oh, wait," the dental assistant says and leaves to fetch what I assume will be paperwork.

Keeping one eye on Emily, I scan the arrayed magazine covers with their anxious questions and concentrated images: they ask, "Is Freud dead?" as puzzle pieces from his face drift toward the margins. If Freud's dead, I want his glasses. They're way cool. Another magazine asks, "Whatever happened to the great American job?" A black-and-white image of a man from the fifties leaps over the headline. Someone had a good day when they thought of these elegant, energetic, provocative images; someone had a better day when they saw them printed, in a newsstand.

"She's ready now," the assistant says. I move toward Emily.

"Like I said, I'm fine. Just spot me," she says.

I nod and follow her, with my eyes focused on her shoulders and my body in a ready position, like a wrestler. Or a second baseman. She's right. She should have called Porter.

The assistant opens the doors. When it looks like Emily is going to open the car door for herself, I surge ahead, open it, and place my hand on her back to guide her in. She ignores my hand, plops into the front seat and announces, "Don't make more of this than it is."

I say, "I'm not sure what that means, but sure."

I know exactly what she means: I am not to infer any greater relationship. We drive silently to the emergency room until I ask for the directions the dentist's assistant has written down. "Turn here" and "get in the right lane" save the silence from being too fraught.

I sit in the waiting room while they check her out and a woman in a Minnesota Vikings-themed radiation vest takes x-rays. The staff appears to check me out and I figure they may somehow suspect domestic abuse, that they are always on the lookout for the inconsistencies and implausibilities in seemingly innocent stories that involve a bruised face and that every glance is forensic. I remove my one glove, so they can see my nice guy knuckles. It occurs to me, with a slight start: there are people in this city who get beat up. Punched, bruised, broken, concussed. Here, in this town, today. My morning victimization consisted of a poorly calibrated conversation confirming that someone I assumed wasn't attracted to me wasn't attracted to me.

Emily emerges. "I'm okay. They just want me to follow up with my doctor."

The bruises are purple swooshes. It looks like she was beaten up by Nike. Her lips are plumped, shiny, and cracked.

There's less fraughtness in the car, but it hasn't evaporated. As she gets out, she starts to say something, to try to revise and clarify what had been said earlier, but it isn't quite happening, so I say "See you on Monday" so she can close the car door and retreat to her apartment. Once there, she fumbles and, apparently, swears. It takes her forever to get in the door.

2

One of Serenity's big things is "service evaporates self," and when
you are damaged enough, or self-pitying enough, basic human con-
sideration counts as service. Since my particular self is so easily
wounded and boring and, from what I can tell, such a pain in the ass,
I think it might be a good idea to stop and buy presents at the Bibelot.

The Bibelot is a gift shop which is so filled with the colors called
chromatic neutrals—organic green Christmas ornaments, wheat-col-
ored paper, yolk-colored candles, aubergine piggy banks—that it
feels like a way-too-precious garden, but there's just enough of a toy
store in its soul to keep it from being totally diabetic. It is where my
friends and I go to buy gifts for each other. It is where we buy the
things that make our forgettable apartments into human places. I like
it there; I like any place you can inventory. I browse the magnetic
poetry which people stick on refrigerators, the Curious George lunch
boxes, the blank journals, the tiny silver or jade vases, the hand-milled
soaps, the satchels of potpourri, the rocks adorned with aphorisms,
the household objects with opinions, all the while thinking of my
friends—my new friends, my old friends with whom I have lost touch.

I immediately grab some wrapping paper with a jazzy neo-Bull-
winkle motif, an off-white festive with muted purple and orange
shapes that resemble paper clips determined to self-actualize.

Looking for something for Porter, I scan for something Christian—he's one of the few churchgoers I know— but there's nothing in this secular store on this secular street. I wonder if the strange greyhound incident provides any clues. No, it doesn't. Then, I find one of those colored leather baseballs. Decades away from his high school glory, he still loves to watch it on his sad little black-and-white TV. They have a bunch of these gift baseballs and, because he grew up in Wisconsin, not far from Minnisapa, I find one in Milwaukee Brewers blue and gold. The ball is perfect. You hold it and a game condenses around you.

The game which condensed for me is pleasant but incidental. Me, I was a more earnest than gifted ballplayer, but good enough to enjoy it as a kid and then again as a grown-up, as the right fielder on Math Anxiety, our agency's team, our excuse to swat and run outside together on beautiful summer nights and then drink in friendly unchic bars. We favored a Polish supper club that was what people who had never seen Las Vegas might think Las Vegas would look like.

For Porter, baseball represents an alternative history—a few years in the minors, a cup of coffee in the bigs—a history in which he had not walked through land-mined rice paddies, in which he had not killed, in which he knew prosperity and praise. Baseball is for Porter what design is for me: elegance in an inelegant world, elegance which runs so deep you could confuse it with meaning.

Emily is harder to buy for and our recent exchange further complicates things, especially since those of us in group treat each other with some tenderness. No one wants to be the cause of someone else's stumble back into failure and disconnection. Thus, I reject a beautifully ornate Santa ornament (too public—she'd be asked where she got it and, though we were friends, she seemed to be constantly dispelling the possibilities that we might be more than friends), a sun catcher with a mirror in the middle (like the Santa, but year-round), and a journal with handmade paper (close, but too personal—it would somehow involve me with her intimacies). Oh, look, some magnetic poetry. Maybe I'll spell out, "This doesn't mean anything." "Oh, the hell with it," I say, tired of envisioning how Emily could minimize me, and I hand the magnetic poetry to the cashier.

I visit the gym because whatever else lifting weights and running on a treadmill is, it is not complicated and it is not subtle and it does not have to be navigated and analyzed and negotiated and processed and strategized. It dispels the mundane poisons of life. I dress in saggy gray workout gear I've always intended to upgrade and descend from the locker room to the club, catching the whiff of chlorine, the smell of sweat, the slamming weights and grunting bodies, the cheerleader yelps from the aerobics floor, and the sight of the fit girls in their teal and mauve and black.

As I work my way around the nautilus machine, I simplify into my body. I simplify into actions: pulling weights down over my head or pushing them away from my chest or rowing them toward my torso. I tense cables and slam weights. My muscles strain and sweeten. My pulse insists within my chest. I hear my breath.

I speak to no one. There are the usual incursions of misunderstood personal space and iffy taste: Some guy who more or less lives here panting too loudly and pacing too close. And yes, the guy on the Stairmaster next to me plays his Walkman so I could hear his awful '80s dance mix. I wish him great pain.

But when I leave the club I feel clean. The world streams deftly through my eyes into my brain. My calf muscles pleasantly ache; I breathe in the chilled, moist air and walk to my car. I feel better, for a while. I feel simpler, for a while.

At home, I wrap the gifts while it is still a simple act.

The baseball for Porter I place in a confetti nest in a red Chinese take-out box which has been wryly repurposed and then I wrap this with a ribbon, tie the bow, feather the bow. I worry the metal handle and then let it be.

The magnetic poetry for Emily comes in a rectangular box. Measure, cut, fold, tape, done. No bow.

Through the gifts I have chosen, I have successfully told people, I love you but not too much.

3

Saturday I spend alone, with my couch, my TV, my refrigerator, my bathroom. The resulting silence is neither friendly nor clean.

4

I find myself without plans on Saturday night, and long after one has gotten used to being alone again on a Tuesday or Wednesday there is something about being alone in your apartment with just your thoughts and your stuff on a night when the rest of the world is presumably off experiencing these great moments in clubs or parties or theaters. Somewhere, not here, music pulses; conversation effervesces; colors flash. Saturday night is when life gets as close as it will ever get to the condensations and glosses and perfections of design.

It is Saturday night and I want to be—I feel a sort of obligation to be—out: to let the sky-blue and black tiles in the First Avenue men's room suggest that I'm drunker than I am by vibrating in some way that I've never quite figured out. (Does the distant, dissociated, rioting band have something to do with it? Does sound nudge color?) I want to puzzle at some bright snarky thing on the Walker Art Center's wall; I want to sink into the balcony seats at the Uptown theater while giant beautiful faces and charismatic apartments or stylized criminals appear on the screen.

Yes, I am this shallow, but my recent misfortunes have apparently done nothing to upgrade my soul. I keep wishing that my failed shallowness was actually depth, but it's not. After forty days in the desert,

I have not achieved enlightenment. I just really want to go dancing or see a movie.

That said, even my criticism of my own shallowness is a little fake. On those excursions into the stylized city, I was searching for some gift that had nothing to do with what I could I say to impress someone around a water cooler on Monday morning, I was searching for some gift which was its own radiant self-sufficient thing, like the birch bark and thistle flowers and milkweeds I brought back from the New Luxembourg pastures when I was five as gifts for my mom. I love the Walker Art Center and the Uptown Theatre because they each grant permission to just look at something for the sake of looking at it, not for the sake of using it to make a point or make a sale.

I want to attend a party where I know some but not all of the people, and I want the kaleidoscope of such parties to align me with strangers who soon feel like friends; I want to be shown that the world is full of sympathetic, interesting souls; I want a life so rich I can't see its edges. My life is nothing but edges; my life is a phone booth. And, on those lost Saturday nights, I was not just searching for something, I was searching with someone; and I miss not having her with me, sounding her humane bass line. *This is beautiful: I want you to have it; I want you to experience it with me; I want it to become a part of who we are.* But what had been "us" is now just "me." This year, even the pronouns hurt.

Sitting here alone, hearing the chorus of the December wind and the people in the apartments next door leaving on dates, hearing the slight wavery excitement of women walking in heels on ice, and watching my Dinty Moore beef stew dejectedly bubbling in a saucepan, I don't want to think about those first weeks with Franny, when we didn't even leave her apartment sometimes because we just wanted to stay in and have sex, even though it meant forfeiting tickets and leaving sheepish messages on the answering machines of friends who'd invited us to their party. I don't need the memory of that desire. I don't need it at all.

But we have not spoken since she moved out, six months ago.

So here I am.

The absence is both arctic and electric.

The absence in my apartment has allowed all my doubts and sadnesses to thrive and vibrate.

Even now, when I've spent months cauterizing what I once felt for her, when every call I don't make to her impacts itself in my soul, even when I hate her for making me hate her, even when she has been nothing but a silence, I still want to call her, but I don't. She said when she left, this has to be clean. Otherwise, it will just be one of those messy not-quite-friendships where we have sex in a moment of weakness.

So.

Sometimes you spend the night with a woman you love; sometimes you spend the night with the TV.

I keep the TV on, for distraction or, I guess, company. What's worse, as I sit, squeezing the remote like I could get it to produce something better, flipping through the channels, too aware of the deficiencies of my futon couch and the cheapness of my recently acquired fake-wood TV stand, I happen upon the Bangles video of "A Hazy Shade of Winter." I usually think music videos are a mess. The whole point of music is that it suggests something subtler than any image or any story could possibly visualize and adding low-rent surrealism and some lame quasi-mimed story to a song is like dressing up a dog. If music and dogs cannot be what they are, if music and dogs are not sufficient by themselves, then the universe needs to be rethought.

Despite this prejudice, I kind of like "A Hazy Shade of Winter";
for once a video has actually caught some of the energy of a song and
possibly the entire movie (*Less Than Zero*), a movie which I'd been
warned off of by the dismissive intelligentsia in the next cube. But Saturday night, with the wind howling in the alley behind my back and
the molecular sadism Minnesotans call "temperature" slowed but not
blocked by the window, "A Hazy Shade of Winter" compresses into
a little over two minutes everything my life is not. Bangles' videos
were always shot so that they were essentially a carousel of the four
pretty women in the band. This one is set in a Los Angeles club, with
cuts to rich kids in various types of photogenic dysfunction, people
making out in convertibles, the artful beard stubble of Robert Downey
Jr's passed-out face, emerald lawns, bedrooms like clouds, twenty
kids encircling a pool with a sort of conga line, hands on each other's warm bodies. The band plays on a stage fitted out with hundreds
of television screens; a blue filter saturates everything so that even
the air is stylish, and the panning camera work captures the feeling
of being perfectly buzzed, confident and fluid. The song rocks like a
thrill ride, with pauses and ascents and accelerations.

The video's from sometime in the '80s and I remember thinking then, when I was watching it with a woman, or at least with a
woman in mind (this is before Franny), "'Time . . . time . . . time, see
what's become of me'? Are they kidding me? Aren't the people in this
movie about twenty-two and rich?" It was the kind of observation
you banked to share with a woman. Now there aren't any women left
to impress.

Or maybe, when I was working at Jay Latir's, I would have noticed
the guitarist, who strutted around like Madonna but who, unlike
Madonna, actually seemed to be enjoying herself, and been reminded
of some car ride from Jay's offices in the suburbs to downtown for
some art directors/copywriters club bash, five of us in the car, two
women who looked great in the jangly, business-tribal fashion of the

time, everyone laughing so hard not at some isolated joke but at some fantastic sequence of giddiness, some series of detonating inflections and shared absurdities. I remember feeling the pleasure of a night out with attractive women without the pressure of a date. We laughed until we actually ached with laughter and phrases from that night could set us off again months later.

But on Saturday I was way past ironic contempt for Hollywood kids singing an old person's song or easy '80s retro fun. The Minnesota December chills the windows and behind my back is an alley with snow as sparse and dirty as rags.

As I watch the video, I keep noticing the bass player, who I'd always vaguely liked: her almost kabuki-white skin, her wine-colored hair, her soft mouth, an interesting ferocity to her eyebrows, but then maybe the faintest, most endearing gawkiness leftover from her pre-rock star days, and something else I unaccountably liked: while she is clearly into the performance, she seems disinclined to vamp for the camera. She is beautiful in a way that implies that she is interesting. She is beautiful in a way that implies that she is kind. I feel a crush beginning. Like I need that.

I am not in high school and I'm not an idiot, although I evidently play one in real life. I know I am staring at a kind of hologram of a woman, I know that beauty seems like enough information but it never is. And yet this lovely image of this lovely woman aches inside me, and she keeps pollinating my thoughts as I sit there watching 50 channels of crap, with each new punch of imagery and sound on the TV, her remembered beauty reminds me of how lonely I am. Whatever is happening on the TV, there is no search, no laughter, no tenderness, no excitement, just so many Doritos of almost-meaning, of junk moments.

What the hell is happening to me? Crushes had become so

harmless Franny and I used to joke about them. We had what we called Approved Crush Lists. Not people we knew, that was dismissed early on as creepy and fraught, but celebrities. This allowed her to make jokes when I hurried in to catch the opening credits of *The Days and Nights of Molly Dodd* so I could watch Blair Brown flirt with New York. When I pointed out that my crush on Ellen Barkin was limited to her early movies, to her odd tentative smile in *Diner* and tremulous beauty in *Tender Mercies*, and that I didn't like her as much when she started taking sexually aggressive roles, Franny could say, "So strong female sexuality frightens you." And I could say, "Hasn't that been obvious?"

The approved crush list allowed me to say, "That's odd. That doesn't look like your kind of movie and yet we're seeing it in the first week. Oh look, it's starring Alec Baldwin." It was like somebody tells you their top five albums, you can triangulate their soul a little.

Those crushes do not ache inside me.

What do I ache for? Not for sex, precisely. I want the sympathy of a touch, the soulfulness of a face, and the enthusiasm in a voice. I am surprised at how little horniness has to do with my crushes and I have always thought this made me freakish, I always thought if I were a more real man, whatever that meant, that I should be always thinking, "I have to nail her." One of the things I liked about my Minnisapa friends is that they clearly liked women—girls, back then—but weren't all crude about it, the way guys were always portrayed as being. It was usually some guy slightly outside of our group who made us realize this: The charismatic-only-to-himself Daryl Ewing once brought some low-rent version of *Playboy* to the bowling alley and I thought it was sad and disgusting, some dull-faced woman spreading her reddened vulva for the camera for money, but I didn't want to say anything. Then Smash Sanborn opened it up and sneered, "Jeez, I don't know, Ewing. I think they need to get the camera a little closer, I can't see her spleen," and tossed the magazine back to him contemptuously. When someone who we knew but who wasn't in our circle asked Pooch Labrador, "Are you a leg man, ass man or tit man?" Pooch said, "I think I'm really a face man." And I'm pretty sure he spoke for all of us, certainly for me, that is why I liked those guys and hung out with them, even though they gave me a different nickname every week. Years later, maybe my last year in art school, I wound up in a bar on Christmas break talking with Quint King, who had been in the navy and said that, if you have enough money, you can get two women to suck your cock at the same time, but that what you really miss is some girl going on about some great book she just read. He said that prostitutes typically do not kiss and they do not make eye contact.

The lovely bassist's face flourishes in me. Outside, someone already drunk spins out on the patchy accumulated snow.

So I sit in the wasteland of my objects: my futon couch, my racks of *Communication Arts* and *Print* and vintage Batmans and Supermans and current X-Mens, my sample files, my CDs and stereo, my angled drawing table and markers, my Brother word processor (Franny had gotten the Mac) my big French 1960s posters and framed collections of 1940s matchbooks.

I sit with my senior year book, where my favorite art teacher, Herb Gould, had signed it, "To one of my best students, ever. I know you'll do great things." Herb himself has done great things, painting local scenes with a delicate realism that people, rightly, loved; teaching a generation of students; raising a family; and, like so many of his generation, serving honorably in an honorable war.

I sit with ambient paper, steel, wood, and cloth.

I sit with the air, the space, the walls, the dark windows.

I sit with the remote and massage my loneliness with images and sound.

When I talked in group about what I lost when I lost Franny, I spoke of a kind of sweetness, and I sensed, especially in Emily, a kind of distasteful shutting down, a smirk and a shrug. I never quite understood this, until once when we were walking to Dunn Brothers, I just asked her, peevishly, what her deal was.

She dragged on her cigarette in a way which reinforced her power—her distance from me, her confidence around men.

"It gets old being dessert."

"Sorry?"

"If you're a woman, or at least if you're a certain kind of woman…." She began in her rapid, highly qualified way. "You know that men view you as the dessert they get for doing well in life."

A much better man would have known what she was talking about. A slightly better man would have asked her to elaborate. I said, "Okay, I can see that," although I didn't. Not really.

And so that exchange died, without me ever quite knowing what she meant or without me ever quite saying what I'd meant. For I'd meant something more than sex or beauty. I'd meant the airy, subtle, everyday joy that makes life livable. I meant something that, despite her beauty, Emily couldn't give me.

It occurs to me now that Franny brought something into my life besides sweetness. She gave me sanity.

Sanity is a tricky thing, that Serenity says we think of as a yes/no when we should think of it as a continuum. And I slide down to a space in the continuum I don't like to inhabit, a place of thoughts becoming obsessions in the cold inner space of my mind in my apartment, of a mind not softly checking and improving another mind just by being in the room, a place without the correction and lift of conversation. I want to compulsively draw the pretty, interesting bassist; and I do and throw the drawings away. I want to go to a record store and buy her band's albums like I was buying pornography, but I don't. Instead, I waste an evening thinking about it.

After tolerating the frat party that SNL had become—you hope you can catch a moment with Phil Hartmann or Jan Hooks—I shut down the nothing that had been this night and went to bed. I lay there in the dark and let my thoughts go where they would. They do not go to the lovely bassist, although I don't know why.

Instead my thoughts go to the scenario with two women that Quint had mentioned and those women were recast as women I know because I lack the imagination to conjure new women, and then they are replaced by Franny, by herself, but this is not a happy reunion, the images flashing in my mind are the opposite of romance, an anger surges through me that I can't stand and can't stop. I grab her shoulder and push her harder when she resists. Near the end, as my breath shortens, and my sternum clenches, as my orgasm begins to solidify and swarm, I can hear drunk people passing below my window, so this suddenly feels shamefully public, yet I can't stop even though I conjure her pinched and pained, helpless and betrayed, and when I come it jolts me like an electric shock, like nothing romantic, like nothing decent, like nothing human, but like a drug I will always need.

The rest of the night is a prison.

EMILY

I scramble from the car of the man who had been nice to me. I grope for my keys in the clutter of my purse—how can someone so poor have so many receipts?—thinking, "my purse does not have my best interests in mind," shivering in the cold-wet-gray—and thinking, "You really can't pass out twice in a day—it's just not done" and then finally locating the damn keys, identifying the appropriate one (slightly bent, fewer notches), and jamming it into the lock and pushing open the door. Because, of course, Duane—why doesn't he change his dorky name?—waits in his car for me to enter the apartment building. As I push, the door grunts open and I lunge into the apartment building's vestibule. I hear him leave.

Thanks to my remark, there's a tension between us.

I actually look at myself in the mirror, which now has the very special insights of the mug shot, and say, "You've made some bad choices." Fortunately, my apartment is a slightly better version of myself: a faded oriental rug, bookcases my father built for me—he wanted to be a woodworker, not a doctor—a tea service. To look at my apartment, you'd think I lived in Bloomsbury and wrote mannerly Avant Garde novels. You would not think that I assault people in department stores with perfumes, clean up the piss and shit of the warehoused old, and regret things. To remind my current chaotic self of my deepest best self, I go to my bookshelf and pull out an Edith Wharton and a George Eliot. I open each in turn and find sentences into which my shapeless, static-filled, suffering self can escape. The sentences themselves almost do not matter, not now. They are places where I can go. "The preamble was felt to be rather long, and several besides Solomon shook their heads pathetically, looking on the ground; all eyes avoided meeting other eyes, and were chiefly fixed either in the spots in the tablecloth or on Mr. Standish's bald head, excepting Mary Garth's." I close the book and, rather than opening the Wharton, I grip the Eliot.

When I've relaxed my grip, and am looking around the room, I feel as if I've been gone longer than I should have been.

I make tea. It's like a tutorial on how to calm down and act decently. I do not sabotage or manipulate the kettle and liquid and bag and cup. I do not pre-empt or offend here in this empty apartment. Let's start with that.

PORTER

I return to my dogless life, driving up Snelling Avenue and then descending to my basement apartment near the freeway, to its stacked newspapers and videotapes and rabbit-eared TV and unopened mail and not-yet-discarded cans of pork and beans and spaghetti-os and soup and SPAM still shamed by their residues and dusty foil packets of macaroni and cheese. Once again, the reactions of others—Emily, Duane—let me know the place stinks a little. All my life, it is the reactions of others which have told me that where I lived was squalid.

But for a dog those smells would be a wonder. For a dog, curiosity shapes their day. For a dog, loyalty shapes their heart. If there was a dog there to share your sleeping and your TV watching and the movements of your mind through the day, that would be something. If there were eyes that saw and spoke to you and a warm body that liked to be snuggled, that would be something. If you could take a dog and make her know that she didn't have to be scared, that would be something. But it will not be something for me.

The Aftermath of Brainstorms

1

Back at the agency, in the days after Franny and I had reunited, we'd landed our biggest account, a bank with offices in twelve states. We partied, a verb I typically hate but, since Brian actually danced with a window shade on his head, I'm okay with it. We hired people.

We presented a campaign we loved—"The most important thing in your wallet isn't your money"—inspired by the wallets of the old guys in New Luxembourg and Minnisapa, and Brian's neighborhood in Saint Paul—some ticket from a Glenn Miller show, a kid's photo, a faded note. The client VP said, "Yeah, that's really nice, it's got legs." And underneath it all was some solid thinking: banks are really in a commodity business—you can't really add features to money. So, you win over customers by being more charming.

The president of the bank was walking by and our client, in a fit of enthusiasm flagged him in. The president looked at it and didn't say anything.

He looked like the guy who made Jimmy Stewart's life hell in every 1940s movie. His facial features looked like they were the result of a conscious decision to become more effective: the steely agile eyes, the efficient baldness, the visible skull. He had frightened his hair, so it fled.

Then he said, "We're a goddamn bank. This ad says banking isn't important. Who did this?"

I said, "The whole agency worked on this, but the line is mine."

"Really. You think you should advertise a bank by saying money isn't important?"

"That's not quite what it's saying. It's saying, 'We're your friend.'"

"We're not your damn friend. We're your bank."

He was comfortable with uncomfortable silences.

Finally, he said, "We're not going to do this. Come back with something serious." Our contact shrugged, simultaneously agreeing with his boss and apologizing to us.

That night, I walked in and started ranting in the direction of Franny. That wasn't unusual. Advertising is a frustrating business. Amateurs get to smudge, dilute, distort, and compromise pretty much everything, and even when they make it better (as they, in retrospect, often do) it usually doesn't seem better. So you need to vent a little when you come home.

Franny asked me how the pitch went as I entered the door and I started on my story about the bank president before I got my jacket off.

"How insulting is that? He just walks in. He knows nothing. I mean nothing. This is the first he's heard of this. He just dismisses two weeks' worth of work. I mean, I can deal with criticism; it's a part of the business; it makes the work better." I probably didn't believe this bit about constructive criticism. I had to say it to convince myself that I was reasonable, which gave me permission to rant: "But the contempt in his voice, the dismissiveness." Franny nodded.

What the client did seemed so unjust that I had to repeat it to myself. Again and again and again.

It was as if I were giving instructions to the world: this is what you need to know, world. Otherwise, everything will be unfair all the time.

"I mean, really, the dismissiveness and contempt. That clown didn't add anything to the process. That kind of attitude just demoralizes people."

Franny said, "Yes, yes, I suppose I can see that. Do you want to maybe take your jacket off and sit down?"

"And then Brian. He just caved. One setback and we're no longer thinking about the best solution for the client. We're trying to guess what will make this jerk happy."

Then, when I was in mid-sentence, she blurted: "My day was just fine, thanks for asking. Or maybe it wasn't."

"Sorry. What?"

I'd expected sympathy, but she was angry. "The person I love isn't just a repository for my anger. I have bad days now and then too. And, you know what, when I have a really bad day I will sometimes sit in my car and scream and sob before I come in because I love you and I don't want to burden you with all my crap."

"What. That's just weird. And I never asked you to do that."

"So I don't get any credit for being considerate—because you didn't request that particular kindness."

"Well, no. But you can't hide something from me and then yell at me when I don't notice."

"You've never noticed that I, like, almost never rant?"

"I just didn't think you were mad about anything. I didn't know you were making a big sacrifice."

"I work in the *legal system* on behalf of *poor people* and you don't think I get mad?"

"Of course, you must," I said. But I was still mad at her.

"Don't you realize what you're doing to me. I'm just this repository. And then you get going and you just take the oxygen out of the room."

"Sorry to, you know, hog the oxygen. I thought that listening sometimes was a part of a relationship."

"It's not sometimes. It's pretty much all the time, Dew." Love had softened and shortened Duane to Dew.

"I'll work on this."

"It's just that, well, I'm sorry. I know it's not about me, sweetie. You want to yell at everyone. But I'm the one who actually gets yelled at."

"I really will work on this. I'm sorry."

"I know. I know."

And yet, every night when I came home—frequently late, always after her—affronts tickled in my throat. And, despite my best efforts, I indulged my tendency to rant. I cut back, but I was amazed at how hard it was to stop. It all seemed so important—every headline, every visual, every finely adjusted visual hierarchy so the ad clicked perfectly in the audience's mind.

A week later, we presented another campaign: bad friends, great bankers. It showed bankers blathering about interest rates at parties, calculating cost-benefit analyses at poker games, and going on about the opportunity cost of fishing. The tagline was, "We're boring friends. We're great bankers."

I could see the impatience gathering in the president's eyes.

I said, "What we did was, we built this on something you said, which is that we're not the customer's friend. We're their banker."

He leaned forward. "I said it. I didn't intend for it to become an ad. I don't think you've done your work here. You just took what I said and gave it back to me."

Our contact came to our defense, redeeming himself a little: "I'm not sure this is the way we want to go, but they have clearly put some work into these commercials. They did build three spots around that line."

Brian said, "Maybe we can talk a little bit about the thinking that was behind your comment last week. We thought it was a very fruitful observation."

The CEO leaned even farther forward, waving away Brian's comment, and said, "Banking isn't complicated. There are four words that matter here. Trust. Integrity. Experience. Judgment. You show those words. You show the definition. You show our logo. That's your commercial."

On the way to the car, I said, "A definition ad. Like that's never been done before. That's so lame in so many ways I couldn't even start to respond."

Brian said, sinking his face in his hands and breathing deeply, "Maybe we can do something with it. We don't have a lot of choice," Scott, our CFO, kept his eyes adamantly on the road.

"He doesn't want us to do anything with it. He wants us to do what he says." The car ride was silent. When we arrived at the agency parking lot, Brian grabbed the boards from the back seat as if they were a gun I couldn't be trusted with. He kicked the car door shut.

I now realize that Brian was every bit as frustrated as I was. He was just a grown-up. He kicked that car door because something in him had been devalued, too. He'd been reminded who had the money and who didn't, too.

We didn't speak on the way back into the building. The elevator percolated our silence.

I was so mad, I just stared at my drawing board for a half hour before going home. I stopped by Brian's and said, "I can't think about this anymore. I'm going home." We took pride in our long hours, especially when we were pitching something. We were hunters, stalking the beast whose entrails would feed the tribe, or, in our case, stalking the clients whose checks would provide us with espresso machines, ironically sophisticated macaroni and cheese at expensive restaurants, museum memberships, and self-esteem. Or, in Brian's case, whatever it is that children need. Hunters who abandon the party get ostracized. I knew all this but I just couldn't think any more.

I boarded the elevator with the receptionist. A bicycle messenger rushed off and asked us to hold while he picked up a package. In the time it took him to do that, Brian walked by the elevator, saw me, and grimaced.

When I arrived at home, Franny was sitting on the couch in a robe, eating cereal. She looked weirdly flustered and awkward, as if I'd surprised her. It did not occur to me that she was also home a little early. I tried to stop myself, but couldn't. The words kept gushing and repeating as if the sheer flood of them could create a new and better world. I knew this was no good, I knew that Franny was probably a little miffed, but the rush of righteous words felt not good, precisely, but distracting, luminous, about to become good, the world felt like a code that trembles just before it resolves itself into language. Franny's eyes hardened and she said, "I was right. I so didn't want to be right."

I said, "What?"

"I stayed home today and when I heard you coming in I returned to the exact same position I'd been in when you left. Look at this cereal. It's been in the fridge all day. I stopped eating it when you left. I'm in the same bathrobe. I'm in the same position on the couch. You didn't even notice."

"You tricked me." I felt shame, but through some sort of dishonest emotional combustion, I could feel my shame become anger. I decided to go the full fuck you: "I don't think I want to be constantly on the lookout for some what's-wrong-with-this picture game you set up."

She quieted and said, as she was beginning to cry, "Pretty much everything's wrong with this picture, honey."

This froze me. I moved in to comfort her. She shook her head at me, to wave me back, and then curled up on the couch.

I just stood there because this horrible stasis was the best outcome I could hope for. Her grievance radiated and accused.

She stared at the floor and hugged herself. "I really love you, but we are thinking of getting married and buying a house. I can't do that with you."

I was silent for a long time. Over on the couch, she was silent too. Implications hardened in the air around us.

Finally, I said, "I think I'm going to go to a hotel. Is that what's best? Is that what you want?"

"Yeah, I think so," she said into the couch.

I just stood there, for longer than I wanted. "I do really love you."

"I love you, too," she said into the pillow. "But it's over."

"I know."

Just a second before, I felt I couldn't move. Suddenly, I did not want to stop moving. When thought becomes horrible, movement becomes strange; it protects you like a scream. I rushed to the bathroom; I jammed a razor and shaving cream and a brush into a Dopp kit I'd extracted from beneath the sink; I lurched into the bedroom, yanked button-down shirts and pressed khakis and a sport coat from the closet; hangers panicked like birds then murmured; I pulled two pairs of boxers and two pairs of socks from drawers; the door didn't shut all the way, so I swore at its maker; I pulled an overnight suit bag from the closet, threw it down on the bed; and hung the shirts, pants and sport coat; I stuck the Dopp kit, socks and underwear in the bottom of the bag.

I knew Franny now wanted me gone. I didn't want to force her to hold her pose on the couch forever. Perhaps the realization that I was being kind to her—that I was being a chump—added to my anger. I pointlessly slammed the bedroom door as I emerged. She was facing me, standing near the door. She looked at me with a sad, tender, slightly scared face.

"You don't need to rush. You can take a few minutes."

With the bag over my shoulder, I could feel the anchoring weight of the Dopp kit and shoes strain my tricep and bounce against my leg.

I wanted to say, "Sure, now that you've won, you can be kind." But I didn't. The tears streaming down her face suggested that she wasn't about to do a victory dance any time soon.

"I'm fine. I have everything," I said. With that, I left.

But the movement which felt like a scream kept me moving. I did not check into a hotel that night. I drove and drove around the metro, 35E to 494, 494 to 100, 100 to Highway 12, Highway 12 into Minneapolis, and then through a half dozen neighborhoods and then back to the block outside our duplex, because I lacked the imagination to park anywhere else, because that place I could no longer enter still had the radiance and magnetism of home. Franny was there.

I thought of when I was a kid and you would hear of people discarding dogs, taking them out on a country road and abandoning them. Would they find their way home and knowing they were no longer loved, still stare at that home that didn't want them?

I slept in the back seat with an animal's unease at the ambient sounds with my neck cramped and my knees floating off the seat's edge. I startled awake because of some urgency in the dream that felt like it was outside the dream, some sigh and caw and smack, and as I shook awake and sat up in the back seat, I saw Franny standing at the bottom of the steps, looking at my car, seemingly full of sadness. She considered walking over to greet me, but didn't. She got into her car and left.

2

Now, I see that in those last weeks, in the build-up to our split, I spent too much time honing my misanthropy in rush hour or dehydrating in some conference room or pacing and strategizing and shrinking the world to the size of my grievances. I spent too little time thinking, "You are wonderful. The world is wonderful." And I'd missed something big. Some sadness had drifted into her, and she had been calling in sick or leaving work early. Was this bleakness that drifted into her the same thing that drifted into my soul now? This sadness with the confidence of a disease and the charm of a drug? That is what she wanted me to notice. The most special three words we can say to another human being are not, "I love you." They are, "How are you?"

The less said about the next month the better. I beached myself at the Saint Paul Radisson for a week. I slept poorly on strange beds—the glossiness of a hotel bed, the pastiness of a futon. I bruised my skin and strained my muscles moving into this apartment. I drank so much Diet Coke my joints hummed. I wanted to focus on work but couldn't. The time I spent working had itself always been pure, a sort of ideal industrious childhood. But now my work time was poisoned by a vaporous, baffling inability to focus. I found myself staring at my drawing board and then retreating from it as if from an abyss:

its whiteness swarmed and snickered. I took to making up administrative tasks and getting lost in pointless unbillable doodles. My mind puddled for hours, then panicked. Despite a constant, neurotic need to move things around, in an impulse that was house-cleaning's crazy cousin, my office became messy and every bit of mess signaled some confusion, some laziness, some micro-paralysis.

And so: sleep deprived, shamed-soaked, roiling with anger, suffering from whatever spiritual dehydration that hotel rooms and bachelor apartments inflict, I picked fights with my partners.

Brian stared across his desk. "You want us to say: we are willing to put people's jobs at risk for work Duane here finds more personally fulfilling."

His desk pushed at me like a Sheriff's belly. His office walls felt emphatic, felt like they were in on it: I swear: they creeped in a couple of micrometers. "We understand you're going through a lot. But if we all did what we wanted here, people would lose their jobs. Yes, at some point I think: those jobs are more important than doing an ad that wins awards." The "we" bothered me more than anything. I wasn't a part of it. It was a bully of a pronoun.

"That's not fair," I said. "This isn't about awards. This is about doing the best possible work for the client."

"Ultimately, the client gets to be the judge of that."

I agreed with him in that I couldn't see a way to disagree with him.

Back at my drawing board, I countered with apathy. Apathy, it turns out, is sluggish but not serene. I wrote the first of the four words the client had dictated—trust—on a sketch pad in big three-dimensional letters. I colored them in with markers; the letters T R U S and T were as substantial as a building. I drew a bird flying over them and squirting a poop onto their vulnerable horizontals. I surrounded them with an asylum of doodles, little 1920s businessmen in bowlers and fangs, abacuses that became jail bars, money bags that metasta-sized into tits or testicles, safes with exposed carnivorous gears, spiked dollar signs menacing various innocents.

Brian walked past with a junior creative team and quipped, "Seems a little off brand." They laughed with him. I sat still and waited for them to pass.

3

I walked into Brian's office. I said. "OK, I'm ready to focus now. The presentation's in four days. Let's nail this thing."

He didn't speak right away. Instead, he contorted his mouth in a way that indicated that certain unpleasant thoughts were sorting themselves in his head. He assumed the look of a man who knew what he had to say but wanted to make sure he said it correctly. He also looked like a man who was annoyed at me for making him have to take such care. "You can certainly work on this. But I don't want you to feel any pressure. Jamie and I have some ideas that we feel good about presenting." Jamie was a junior art director whom I had hired.

"I didn't know you guys were working on anything."

"We chatted a little yesterday and worked on them last night."

Oh, no, I thought. "OK," I said.

"Still, I've been thinking about this. I'd like to take a shot at this."

"Sure, the more ideas the better." Brian said. This meant that my ideas were gratuitous. I was like a child at an amusement park who actually thinks he's steering the little boat.

"Is there some reason you guys didn't share anything with me?" I tried, not very hard, not very successfully, to keep the hurt and irritation out of my voice. Agencies are rivers of information: notes, creative briefs, white boards filled with the aftermath of brainstorms, sketches, concept boards, pink while-you-were-out slips, drafts, drafts flagged with post-its and scrawled with marginalia, estimates, timelines, proposals, slide shows, color separations which magically constitute the world from cyan, magenta, yellow, and black, proofs, samples. Agencies are a swirl of things becoming better things.

"We were planning to. They're still being fleshed out."

"OK," I said. "I'm going to think about this tonight. I'd like to work alone for a while. I'll check in with you in the morning."

"Sure."

I was so hurt I couldn't think. I could feel the hollow under my eyes where tears wanted to be. I wanted to kick Brian's ass, to come up with great work. And this put tremendous pressure on every idea. There are very few ad concepts so good they qualify as revenge. I demanded greatness, but I couldn't stand the merely good and often goofy ideas that always are a prelude to great. I know that creativity is supposed to be about passion, but you also need a kind of lightness, a sense that ideas are just popcorn and nerf balls and silly putty. That's why we use all that crap, to reassure ourselves that this is play, to cut ourselves the slack we cut children. And then you also need to know that at some later point ideas will be taken seriously. But the opposite was happening here: these ideas mattered too much to me now; they would matter too little to Brian later.

I stayed with it. I eventually came up with some things. What if you pushed the clients' suggestions as hard as you could visually? For the word, "security": a child on a windy city street, holding his mother's legs. No, her mother's legs. You couldn't squirm out of the clichés but maybe you could reinvigorate them. Maybe you could cast just the right talent and capture just the right expression; maybe, you could style, crop, filter. Make them human, make them stories, make them surprises. And that pointed to something that might be a solution and that subtle, sudden alignment of my thoughts made me happy for the first time in weeks.

That rough layout of that child hugging her mother's leg would be the last work I would do for the agency I helped found. The next morning, Brian approached me as I stood at the coffee pot.

"Do you have a second?"

"What now?"

He hesitated and his voice was even quieter.

"To talk about something in my office." We walked silently.

When we both sat down, also silently, he paused.

"We've been through a lot together," he said. "We can never deny what you gave to this place." He was crying without acknowledging it; his eyes were misting and leaking. "But it's not working out."

He waited a second while I translated "it's not working out" into "you're fired." I didn't protest. We were past arguments.

He said, "It's no one thing, and it's been building for some time."

"I know," I said.

He breathed in, then proceeded. "There's a severance package and a non-compete. Scott is going to run you through those. You can take every-two-week payments or you take a lump sum at a percentage." Scott entered the office, which became small. He bumped past me as tactfully as he could and nodded to both of us at once, as if to acknowledge our history as partners.

Both he and Brian seemed ugly and noble. Brian, fleshy, strong-browed, block-headed; Scott, with his thrifty, girlish features. Each seemed like an odd lonely primate you glimpse at a zoo. I'd almost never seen them in repose, or sad. They'd usually been happy, hale fellows, or at least animated enough by whatever crisis the agency was going through.

"I'll take my lump, if it's not going to hobble you guys." What a time to make a pun. And what an odd residue of partnership. Partnership is an emotion, a kind of love. Why was I looking out for the firm that fired me?

"No, we've done all the math here. It is cleaner that way."

The non-compete was for one year. The compensation was adequate—well, adequate to get me through the year and maybe a few months of job hunting.

"What about cleaning out my desk?" I asked. I couldn't bear putting my things in a box while people awkwardly watched. Not again.

"We are thinking maybe you could come in tonight. We'll tell people that some work is being done in the offices, so that no one's around. The word today is that you are visiting a potential client in the outstate."

There was a sign above the creative department, which I glimpsed, distantly, as I left: *Never confuse raised voices with high standards.* Brian had written it as a reprimand to some of our screaming bosses in the past. I'd sent it to the typesetters and then finessed what they sent back. It hadn't taken more than a quarter hour but the type was perfect. The ligatures were considered.

We were going to be different. I focused on the sign Brian and I had created and left the faces of people working at their boards blur.

I started to sob in the elevator.

EMILY

Saint Paul became my geographic cure. I know, you've all told me
that is just a way of running away from my problems. Well, America is a world-historical geographic cure. If running away was good
enough for our ancestors, it's good enough for me.

On the morning of my move, I was exhausted—that special
exhaustion where your joints ache from lifting, you've inhaled
a corpse worth of dust, you hate the flaps and edges of boxes, you're
tired of the puzzles of spatial arrangement and weight distribution,
you hate lugging and sliding and shoving, you hate your defamiliar-
ized apartment, and you are pre-exhausted by the prospect of driving
cross-country. On the plus side, you've managed to get the caretaker
to help without sleeping with him.

So that's when Dad shows up and starts hauling furniture and,
in about five minutes, he and the caretaker are buddies. After he
has everything in the car, he is able to spend a full hour repacking
it and securing the roof rack. He keeps shifting things from roof to
trunk to back seat; he keeps sitting in the driver's seat and checking
the sight lines. You are so tired you get mad at him, but he ignores
your anger and says, "Just two more minutes, honey, and I'll have
everything right."

"God damnit, Dad, I need to go."

"Just a minute," he says, calmly, focused on the knot he's re-tying.

"All right," he says, and I hug him and get angry at him for crying.

*   *   *

In Montana, I see a woman by the side of the road, with a trail of her possessions sputtered behind her.

I realize that obsessively securing your load is how a man who can't say he loves you says he loves you.

PORTER

The worst shadows had not been those of Vietnam. I had my brothers there. I'd had the thin garment of patriotism. The worst had been the trickster shadows of a cab. I'd picked him up when I lived in another city, from one of those failed lounges where the light was sickly, seemingly tinctured with blood.

It was after bars were closing, and my fare was drunk, drugged, slurring, and surging. He started to climb out of the cab without paying and I popped the locks. He said, "Oh yeah, I'll fucking give you something."

Please consider the phrase above. When does it mean "I forgot and I'm sorry;" and when does it mean "I will assault you"?

These questions matter. I answered them in a certain way. My passenger died with only his wallet in his hand. Because I had shot him in the throat, he gargled and spit blood which, as I approached his shocked face to help him, spilled all over me. This is what I know of shadows.

Rampant Enoughness

1

When I wake up after my sad Saturday night animated only by a crush on a video woman, the surprisingly sunny winter light feels like grace, if not forgiveness. I try to tell myself, when the shame fights to resurface: dude, you just jacked off. But I know what simmered in my mind.

The Sunday morning light reminds me that somewhere families are driving to church and quieting their kids as the priest intones the death and rebirth of Christ.

Every Sunday in New Luxembourg, the entire town would show up for church. The farm families would come in from the country. And, from our shirts sometimes still warm from the iron to our ancient prayers we mumbled, we were all our best selves for an hour. Well, mostly. We also scanned the pews and gathered material for gossip; we nodded off. But we somehow absorbed talk of miracles which thrilled the world into being. We heard parables of a man who knew that everything was as holy as he was. I missed the walls filled with saints and stories, the angelically filtered light, the offered glossy wafers. I liked communion wafers because they tasted like Elmer's paste—that orange and blue package, that crazy cow head for a logo—which I was not allowed to eat. We were dressed up, we had left the house and gathered with our neighbors, we had also traveled to a place where the 2,000-year-old narrative on the walls pulled us from our petty now and our thin here.

I'd hate to index what happens in the hour I used to spend in a church. I've traded the ancient ritual for half-sleep in my underwear.

Eventually, I drive to the health club because I'm the only self-described yuppie in captivity—after design snob and liar at my temp job and fantasy misogynist last night, what have I got to lose?—and the gym's my real church or at least where my self sweetens into something more graceful.

On the way to the gym, I stop at a SuperAmerica and walk in to pay because I want the human contact and the visual stimulation: beef jerky and single-use aspirin and lottery tickets in bright fluorescent light. A cheerful black kid hands me my change. The idea behind his cheerfulness is wonderful: the best use of the self is as a container for joy. I love the theory—I may have heard it once or twice from one of the nuns—but I don't quite grasp how you actually get past the vague grinding of moodiness, the default wincing and worrying and preoccupation and banality of the soul. And yet the cashier, ten years younger than me, with probably far fewer advantages, has gotten beyond those things. He smiles like he means it.

As I open my car door and get in, I swear I heard someone yell, "Hey," but I look around and see nothing. The voice is familiar: cheery, a sweet solid Midwestern's woman's voice with a few teasing top notes.

I feel clear and strong. But I still have to solve the problem of Sunday, which is to say the problem of lonely, which is to say the problem of empty.

My old friends reappear: The near-wind in the limbs, the near-sickness in the gut, the near-tears in the head. When I return to my apartment, sure enough, the space feels less innocent than before, the day inexplicably shifts into a minor key. The light feels weary. A better man would sit with this; would allow himself to feel the feelings.

I turn on football—a snowglobe of a game, Bears-Eagles, calling up games played as a kid. Snow reinforces that this is play, slippery and padded and flailing; the snow sentimentalizes the game for me in a way that the men bruising and concussing each other would find laughable. The game fizzles. I let it wallpaper the afternoon.

I do laundry—yes, I'm back to doing laundry in laundry rooms. I bring a load of clothes down, balancing the box of detergent on them so I don't spill its candy-bright crystals. A stranger's underwear spins and sloshes in the machine next to me. I jam my clothes, softened by wear, into the washer, add the detergent, insert coins, and leave my underwear to its watery fate. As I'm coming back up the stairs, I realize that writing out Christmas cards might cheer me up, because, unlike more personal overtures, they would probably be well received. You can't really say "fuck you" to a Christmas card. I appraise—or is the right word "apprise?" Brian would know— the possibilities for judgment and misunderstanding in a Christmas card. I also hear the phone ringing as I approach the apartment. The answering machine clicks as I unlock the door. But no message appears. For weeks after the breakup, I would have assumed this would be Franny. But that kind of speculation just exhausts me now. Or, at least, that is what my best self says. My best self is winning more arguments these days, but not all of them.

2

I decide to get provisions. It promises to be definite, practical, multi-colored, and softly aerobic. It may be social.

By walking down to Kowalski's grocery store, I am doing what Serenity suggests--picking up my thighs which pick up my feet which move me through the chilled air and along the sometimes-slick sidewalk. I breathe the air, I see the sky; I note colors (Green awnings! Holy buckets!) and I note architectural form and detail (Cornices! Cornices? Really? Sure.) and the glint of the shops (Jewelry!). I walk across Grand Avenue where another road—a strange, uncompleted spur that seems to serve no one—runs under it. My stomach has a little philosophical flutter as I look down.

I keep walking; the store is near. As I approach, every step enlarges it slightly.

I joke and joke about these therapeutic stratagems of mine but the world emerges and touches my gloveless hands with its chills and fills my eyes with its skies and substance and fills my body with its movement and tug. Serenity is right: the ability to move and to breathe and to notice are the essential gifts.

I tell myself I have enough, although the fact that I'm walking toward a grocery store suggests I technically don't.

Kowalski's reminds me of the grocery stores of my youth, which made Minnisapa seem glamorous. (Yes, people who think of a place with a grocery store as a big city are hicks but in our defense, we were assured that they were super markets and presumably, where Superman shopped.) Kowalski's brings back that feeling of sensible abundance as I walk through the door which has acknowledged my motion and, automatically, Star Trekishly opened for me. And this makes me think of my mom, as I view the armada of carts and mini carts and hand baskets, of all those grocery store trips in Minnisapa when I made life miserable for that poor woman as she tried to feed us properly and I lobbied for TV dinners and bonkers cereals and preposterous olive loaf and occasionally went limp from sheer sensory overload and/or 8-year-old existential fatigue.

In blasé 1993, I grab one of the smaller carts, the kind that didn't exist in the '60s because the '60s were about families the size of presidential cabinets and turn left into the produce section—the bright pyramided apples and oranges, the figs or dates (I can never remember which) in clear plastic containers, the lettuce and red peppers. Nature is a kick-ass package design firm, and this is its portfolio.

And so: taco shells, pickles, yogurt, horrible bagels, cheese and milk and cheese-ish products, pasta sauces, Christmas candies, dozens of SKUs, rampant enoughness, and then the cereal aisle, where all the consumerism gets turned up to eleven—thanks to the madness of packaging, thanks to the madness of people like me who design the packaging. The exclamation marks, the primary colors, the animated characters, the frosted chunks and infused bursts and lacquered nuggets, the more than enoughness, the never enoughness of it all. Someone—a college kid, I'd guess, by the esoteric band t-shirt and scraggly beard and the slight air of bafflement at adult tasks—is paused before a segment of shelving that has garnered his attention, sifting through the adjectives and photographs explaining what he might want to eat today.

And then, there, coming into view, behind the college guy, alone, contemplating a cereal box, is Franny. She looks lovely. She is rotating the box. She is examining it like it is a recently uncovered archeological specimen. The rest of the packaging is chattering around me: the cartoon characters, the giant letters and spoons and, for some reason, race car drivers. This is the year that people cared what cereal race car drivers ate. Amid the clutter and clatter, I think: she's just feet away but I can avoid her.

She is still studying a Cheerios box, in that serene distracted way we have in grocery stores. I approach, drawn to her like a man on a beach might be drawn to water; I micro-strategize what I am going to say, and, prompted by her attention to the cereal box, I go with funny: "What do we really know about Cheerios?" I say. "I mean they were only the first solid food we ever ate." As I say this, I realize it's a stupid thing to say, that it tries too hard, that it's not kind enough, that it doesn't acknowledge what's special about this moment after all these months--that I'm yet again being the guy who values being clever above just about everything else, that I'm being a goddamn ad guy, that I'm being exactly the guy she left.

She turns and exclaims, but softly, "Oh my God."

I can't read her expression, which is to say that she didn't express unambiguous joy at seeing me again.

I go to some pains, to the extent that one can go to some pains in seven one hundredths of a second, to play it cool.

We are silent. We look at each other, almost too directly. She lowers her head and purses her lips. I just stare, hopefully, vulnerable now. Booberry, Captain Crunch, Count Chocula, the Honey Nut Cheerio Bee, the Kellogg's Corn Flakes Rooster, and the Rice Krispie Dwarfs witness this awkward, bottomless, moment.

She gathers her wits before I gather mine. "So how have you been?" she asks. She's tentative, almost tender.

"Good . . . enough," I say. Like a high school kid, I want the pause to say more than the words say; I want her to feel my ellipses; it's my attempt to express the last months, the fullness of their emptiness, the hopefulness of their despair, the richness of their boredom, the strangeness of their normalcy. And, yes, like a high school kid, I'm clueless: I can't explain how this emptiness and detritus may have added up to something.

I want her to think: He's changed. But have I?

And then I say, "You know."

Know what? I'm not sure, exactly. You know that I've hit a bad patch, I guess.

And she said, "I know," with some gravity and sympathy.

We had enough mutual friends that the news of my fall reached her. For the first time in some time, I think: I've been the subject of conversations. Probably not conversations I would have been happy to hear.

"It was so much to happen at once, how are you dealing?" she asks. She's trying to be kind without admitting guilt.

"I don't know. It may all be for the better."

"Really?" she asks.

"I need to view this as a blessing," I say.

"That sounds like a good attitude," she says. A smile thaws her face a little more.

"I'm sorry," I say. "I should have avoided you. You've said you don't want to see me."

"No, I'm glad you didn't avoid me," she said. She seems to stop talking before she's through. She seems to weigh options long before she speaks again. "I'm glad to see you. It's just weird. I'd wanted to be a little more prepared for this."

"Yeah," I acknowledge, "I don't want it to be weird or tricky." I say. "It's hard to see you, but I want you to know that I'm really sorry." Franny looks disturbed. Maybe this was the wrong thing to say, maybe I should have saved this for when we were both more prepared.

No, that's not it. Franny has noticed that a woman with a cart has been standing behind us, glaring at us but not asking us to move. "Oh, I'm so sorry, ma'am."

I move back and Franny moves forward, to let her through. The woman pushes ahead angrily, ending our delicate, tentative conversation.

"I guess we didn't understand the death rays she was sending us," Franny says.

It is an inside joke about Minnesotans who won't say what they mean but instead just stare at you. More importantly, it is our inside joke.

"I guess not," I say.

Thank you, my vague Lord, for this shared joke. Thank you, passive-aggressive Minnesota woman.

But again, the question: what next? It feels like I've just discovered fire and that my one sample is flickering and I'll never get it lit again if I don't do something.

"Okay," I say. "Why don't we meet for coffee sometime."

"Yes," she says. "Let's do that."

This leaves us with an awkward reality: we were both proceeding through a grocery store at roughly the same pace in roughly the same order. If we don't do something, we will keep running into each other.

I say, "Well then I'll go pay for my bananas and milk and call you tomorrow to set something up." I have other groceries to buy but I can live on a pizza for a day or two. Or a week or two. I'm a dude in his thirties, after all.

"Great," she says.

As I walk down the aisle, I look back and smile (she smiles back). As I walk back to my apartment, I am happy, and this happiness feels both ecstatically thrilling and deeply sane. I realize what I should have said to her: "How are you?"

Goddammit.

I decide against running after her.

3

That night, I create my first design in months. There is a line from a poem that Franny loved and read to me, a poem called "Resort" by Patricia Hampl, who lives around here somewhere. "Nothing is perfect except the light falling on imperfection." I arrange the type vertically, one word to a line, to simulate falling snow. I indent words to make the line tumble down the page. I add circles, which imply falling snow. I try it with the words in the circles and outside of the circles. I draw a big circle with a snowflake within it and arrange the line over that. I decide that all of this is wrong, for reasons I can't quite name.

I give up and make cocoa. Absolutely no one is expecting a card from me. I will luxuriate in my irrelevance. As I dispel cocoa pimples, it comes to me:

Go back a step. You don't show the snowflake—way too literal. You imply the horizon. The line needs the elemental confidence of a sunset or sea. I make it horizontal. Increasing the letter spacing calls too much attention to the type and too little to the thought within the type. The intelligence dissipates in the spaces between the letters. I try Helvetica, which is both too aloof and too boring for this. This line requires some commitment, some serifs and thicks and thins.

But Bodoni is too fussy.

Garamond. There we go.

I approximate 20-point Garamond bold with my magic marker. Nice.

But I try it at 36 points, just to see. Nope, it's shouting. At 12 points, it might whisper like snow. Nope, again. The line invokes one of those '70s guys who speaks very softly to convince everyone how sensitive and Dan Fogelberg they are.

And so:

"Nothing is perfect except the light falling on imperfection."

20-point Garamond Semi Bold, tight but not touching, clean, horizontal.

That will be my message to everyone who still loves me or once loved me and is still in my address book. I'll call a typesetter tomorrow, have the type Tuesday, get it to a printer that day, and mail it in a week. It will be late for Christmas but not for the season.

EMILY

I am throwing a party, because why not concentrate all the anxiety of complicated relationships and Christmas and half-assed self-discovery into a ball and throw it at your own head? I've never planned a party. What does one do? Somehow procure a *cheese log*?

And aren't there *activities*? Things you wouldn't normally ever do for any reason except at a party? Existential calisthenics. A piñata stuffed with regrets. Maybe I'll come up with some feats of skill. And maybe whatever else it takes to keep us all from confronting the awful truth that a party is just a bunch of people in a room together. Or am I alone in considering that an awful truth?

I go out and buy some women's magazines, a multi-million dollar industry fed solely by my sense that I missed a memo.

PORTER

My pastor once asked me what I saw in Duane and Emily. To him, they are ironic urban secularists, selfish wayward souls. I love Duane and Emily because they recognize that, when you are trying to sort out a way forward, irony can be a kind of love.

I tried to explain what I meant by this to my pastor, who does not understand irony, but I couldn't make it clear to him. It had something to do with the soul's need for an astringent. It had something to do with acknowledging the imperfection of the world.

Or maybe I should have just said that I like quips made in coffee shops. For a brief time, they make my life feel like a light, joyful thing. There are worse places to live than in sitcoms.

The Optimal Configuration of Regret and Swallowed Annoyance

1

And so, the next morning, still digesting the meeting with Franny, I take a meditative walk through fresh snow along Grand Avenue, a street which, in its gentleness and abundance, always reminds me of Christmas. And so, I happily arrive at the design disaster of Serenity's office—that Sam Spade ascent up the steps, that dry rich smell like what I imagine the 1940s smelled like; and then the milky light through the windows, the ridiculous random pterodactyl/tractor artwork and the Jetson-reject orange teardrop chairs and the battleship desk.

And so, to group.

When I arrive a minute before start time, I spy Porter, looking sad in a way that asks for pity; Emily, looking distant in a way that asks for closeness; an older guy in a polo shirt and khakis that he thinks are casual, with a face that strikes me as shallow and dismissive. I exchange non-committal heys with everyone.

Serenity walks in and anchors himself at the front of our circle. "Okay, let's get started," he says, almost judgmentally, as if our silence were a kind of laxity. Something is bothering him, but since he isn't allowed the flaws and fractals of mood, we won't hear about it.

He introduces the new member, a recently retired executive who, according to Serenity, is having trouble with retirement. I should be able to relate to him, in our mutual nostalgia for commutes and to-do lists and conference rooms, but I am pretty sure I won't. He looks like a bad client—the kind who think they're decisive when they're actually just dismissive, the kind of people for whom decisiveness is a kind of laziness, a failure to consider anything but the easiest thoughts and the most banal facts. The kind that sorta ruined my life, to the extent that anyone other than my sad angry self ruined my life.

Then, two other regulars appear: Jenny, a mother suffering from postpartum depression who shows up five minutes late and apologizes; Trevor, a kid who can't seem to properly start college because the Doors album that plays in certain teenage boys' heads plays especially loudly in his. His widowed mother can't figure out what to do with him. He slouches at the world.

We know Jenny and Trevor. We've heard their secrets. We are not above making fun of them. Not for their secrets, precisely, that would be mean, even for us. But for their more petty delusions, the ongoing self-parody that they called a personality, their genius for being annoying, or, alternatively, our genius for being annoyed. I am practicing taking responsibility for things, even when my responsibility isn't clear. "I am sorry for standing on the sidewalk while you jumped the curb and ran me over." See, that's accepting your part.

We share. Look at us sharing. Jenny has installed something called America Online on her computer and she is using it to somehow correspond paperlessly with other new moms. As I try to imagine what this must look like, she reports what it sounds like: the device—her computer, plus some adjunct device—make an occasionally panicked grinding noise, an electronic gargling and throat-clearing that is starting to get to her. Trevor shares, briefly. He is reading Aldous Huxley, who's apparently a trippy version of Orwell. I share about my weekend, leaving out the hour and forty-seven-minute crush on a set of cosmetically intense pixels and the angry masturbation. My loneliness is noted but not its boring, dirty, beige, beef-stew-and-basic-cable emptiness. My encounter with Franny is noted, more or less accurately, sans digressions about cereal packaging and the social dynamics of grocery stores and the ennui of eight-year-olds.

It is Emily's turn.

"This was an . . . eventful week," she begins, pronouncing the ellipse. Laughter. There's been a lot of pronunciation of ellipses lately. "I had a bad panic attack when I was at the dentist's," she says, "But, I mean, really, it's rational to panic at the dentist, right?" More laughter. "It was all very embarrassing, and, of course, I fell and bonked my nose because I'm the only person in the world who can turn panic into a contact sport." Laughter.

"You're not the only person," Serenity says, almost inaudibly.

"I mean, panic really IS my sport. And because I needed a ride to the emergency room, the incident forced me to reach out in ways that I don't like to reach out. I mean, I'm usually all, 'I've got this.' And that was good. I had my handy dandy call sheet ready and called Duane."

Man, do I hate the phrase "handy dandy."

"So, you know," she continues, "I stretched myself a little. And I like to think that I maintained a sense of humor about it."

"That's true," Serenity said. "Humor is perspective and perspective is good."

I guess what Emily is saying is true in that she states nothing verifiably untrue. But she leaves out so much and softens so much of what she does say that I'm slightly affronted. God, we're bullshitters. What we tell ourselves, in generally photogenic terms, is *I was misunderstood, I was hurting, I was frightened, I was perhaps too passionate. I just cared too much, man.* Granted, when the process works well, all this rationalization-pretending-to-be-analysis hammers through to the vulnerable soul inside and that transforms the room and the hour into a place of empathy and serenity which really does feel like a kind of spiritual oxygen. But we stop short of responsibility. What we do not tell ourselves is: *I was a dick.* Or we say it, we take responsibility, but it's always couched in *I mean well.* Do we? There's always a little gauze of assumed good intentions in group. The group forgives you almost as much as you forgive yourself.

Emily leaves out her unpleasant weirdness toward me, her anxious need to tell me this was only a ride, her hurtful pre-empting of intentions I didn't even have. And if she hadn't been such a damn neurotic, maybe she would have more friends and maybe she would have been able to call someone besides me. We think we're rigorous in group but I'm not sure we are. Or maybe I've just had enough of Emily. After all, would anyone expect her to talk about the strange tension of our encounter?

It is Porter's turn. "Again, Duane was a part of my most important experience this week," he says. I'm coming off as kind of a star this week, although this doesn't make me happy. "As was our platoon leader," Porter continues. He salutes Serenity, who flinches.

"I believe I did the righteous thing," Porter says. When Porter launches "righteous" into the room, the new guy's face quickens with the kind of concern the adamantly normal feel for fanatics who want us to engage with their fanaticism. And the new guy is adamantly normal and who's to say that a life lived between the lines is such a bad thing. Trevor-who-can't-handle-college just rolls his eyes. The "whatever" which is his response to the world has been dialed up slightly.

Porter continues, "I guess the lesson was that doing the right thing doesn't always feel good." He's right. We expect doing the right thing to offer at least a muted satisfaction. Sometimes doing the right thing just yields the best possible mess, the optimal configuration of regret and swallowed annoyance.

As I formulate this, I notice that Serenity has quickened.

"Porter, I want you to note that you said 'righteous thing' a few minutes ago and 'right thing' just now. Think about the difference between the two words. And, second, please tell your story. You cut right to the moral."

"Yes," Porter says. "Here's my story."

This will be good. Porter can make a trip to SuperAmerica sound like the exodus of the twelve tribes from Egypt. And Porter can talk like this without seeming pretentious or like he's trying to get laid. His hurts have been biblical.

"While making a delivery, on a snowy night last week, I spied a greyhound who was lost and who was shivering and who overcame her shyness only because I was delivering hot food. Well, I took on this lost soul and gave her sanctuary in my car and fed her pizza and left the car that night only to use the bathroom because she would weep with abandonment and terror every time I left. I slept in the front seat that night and she slept in the back. I called her Honey, because of her color. She awakened something in me that has been rarely awakened, even when I was a boy. I know you can't fall in love with an animal and I know you can't fall in love in a night. But. . . "

Porter stops. He fights tears.

"Maybe it was that, for once in my life, I was the one with gifts to give."

Porter is having trouble. His heart had been tenderized and broken in the same day. I hadn't been quite aware of that when he'd brought Honey/Caper to Serenity's office earlier this week. Whatever happened in Serenity's office with the dog had felt more mundane than that.

He finishes. He's found the owners and returned the dog. He realizes he never could have kept the dog because his apartment building doesn't allow pets and that he knew that when he drove all night with the dog in his backseat but couldn't bring himself to articulate it to himself.

He's processed his resentment and grief over that, as we say.

Processed, as if these soul dilemmas were cheese.

That, being a dog whose soul fluttered like a candle.

The retiree, whose name is Gary, is asked to share.

"I don't know," he says. Of course, I want to say, if we knew, we wouldn't be here.

But he really doesn't know. He has worked his entire life. He says, with a surprising insight for an old white dude in khakis, "I never realized how useful problems were. I always woke up with a problem to solve. Now, it's suddenly three in the afternoon and I don't know what happened today, only that I'm even sadder than I was when I woke up."

"What if you treated the lack of a problem as a problem?"

"That's a little fancy for me," he says.

"We will always be creatures of tension and struggle. That's the nature of life," Serenity says. This is Serenity at his best. "That's what the principles I've outlined help us address."

He continues. "The need for some tension in the bowstring bedevils many of us. We hate tension and we hate that struggles are the accouterments of purpose and purpose is the whole point. The purpose of life is purpose."

Serenity is getting a little meta for us, and we're used to him. Emily and I exchange skeptical glances. Everyone shifts uncomfortably.

Serenity appears to be building up steam. His knees are bobbing like crazy. Emily mimes dragging on a cig. Porter and I smile. We've devoted some time to imagining what the pre-enlightenment version of Serenity must have been like. We are pretty sure it involved him doing violence to cigarette after cigarette as well as flask after flask and possibly even syringe after syringe.

"That's why heaven has always seemed so problematic. It's atrophy. It's a kind of an abyss of happiness."

Now, Emily mimes smoking a joint. Porter and I try not to react. It is micro-sympathies like these which made us friends, despite our differences. "Abyss of happiness" will get some play if we get a chance to confer after the meeting.

"The problem of death is the problem of work. Either our consciousness just stops. Or it continues but without any agency. Where is the meaning when we stop working? Can there be meaning in just existing?"

We've all moved from amusement to concern. We share small sympathetic looks.

"I'm sorry," Serenity says, reading the room. "We typically stop short of the metaphysical here, Gary. What I can tell you is that we will help you find ways to make your retirement meaningful. Paid work may end but human usefulness does not."

That is the Serenity we know and love.

"And we will also help you find meaning in the quiet times where despair wants to creep in."

"Thank you," Gary says. He is polite. He is also clearly a little flummoxed. So are we, because we know that Serenity battles his own crazy and there are just enough signs that he might not be winning that battle. His words were only a little off but his voice and his knees suggested something was awry.

After group, Trevor comes up to me. I never really engage him outside of group, not even in these moments afterwards where the aura of the group still hangs over us. He says, "Are you worried about Mr. Griffin?" He means Sergeant Serenity.

The "Mr." strikes me. Trevor was a good boy before his father's death and, I suspect, in some ways, he still is.

"A little," I say.

"I don't like the way he's talking. That's a dangerous way to talk. Do we need to do something?"

We all sensed it. But Trevor acted upon what we sensed.

And something in his past taught him that this kind of talk—talk that tempts the abyss—is dangerous.

The Doors album that plays in certain teenage boys' heads is playing especially loud in his. Jesus, what a glib stupid thought. I wasn't one of those troubled boys; my lostness became something tamer, an obsession with the purities of design, but I knew some of them and I knew what they went through, for all its melodrama, was no picnic—a churning of sex and idealism, self-hatred and self-obsession, a frantic attempt to shape and claim a real self before the world forced you into a false self, a sense that you might never meet the secret demands of the universe, whatever the hell they were, washes of anger and horniness that only the loudest music could even hope to resolve, and beneath it the loneliness that comes from your clueless attempts to translate all this into something girls would find charming, the loneliness that comes from the loss so deep it doesn't even have the grace of a loss, that dead father, that clueless rage that was years away from being insight. I look at Trevor and I see Quint King fifteen years ago and I see the same decency poking through Trevor that I saw poking through Quint.

"We shouldn't have to take care of our Counselor, Trevor," I say, as kindly as possible.

"Okay," he says. "But could I have your phone number, in case I want to talk?" he says.

"Of course," I say. We exchange numbers. I still have two old business cards. I write my personal number on one and he writes his on the other.

"Cool cards," he says, admiring the design.

I am now officially a man without a business card. This troubles me more than it should.

A block and half ahead of me, Porter and Emily enter our favorite coffee shop. As I get closer, I can smell the roasting coffee and glimpse the pastry case. Emily and Porter are dumping additives into their coffees. They nod to me and grab a table.

Dunn Brothers was here before the Starbucks and the Caribous and the dozens of one-offs that popped up last year. It has a clientele which liked expensive coffee in European spaces before that was a thing—except, of course, in Europe, where it was presumably always a thing. It has a chalked menu, arrayed battalions of scones and Danishes and muffins, bohemian-attractive and surprisingly friendly counter help, a zillion posters, a thin ordering space made thinner by our puffy winter gear, free weeklies, *The New York Times* (not free), perpetually not-quite-empty thermoses of cream and milk, corrugated cup holders and complex plastic lids, a churning roaster in the corner flanked by lounging burlap sacks of beans, a second counter where you can buy beans from under glass which are then scooped into little brown bags by the staff who then hand write the product and date on, and, finally, a room filled with small tables that are poorly balanced and frequently jostled, which gives the effect of being on a ship at sea. There's a small stage where a lot of singer-songwriter dreams begin and, too often, end.

The place is crowded. Besides those of us who are vaguely recovering, there are a fair number of people here who are specifically recovering. This section of St Paul is an immigrant community for those who've come to Minnesota to cleanse themselves of their addictions to alcohol and drugs. Dunn Brothers does a brisk business in its minor stimulants and legal consolations—not the least of which is human companionship.

When I sit down, Emily says, "So 'abyss of happiness'?"

"Yeah, that was something,"

Emily says, "So can you just attach 'abyss' to, like, anything?"

Porter says, "I think it has to be an abstract noun."

"So, no abyss of Twizzlers?"

"Unfortunately, no."

"You sure?"

"But an abyss of glee."

"An abyss of whimsy."

"An abyss of moderation."

"An abyss of insouciance."

"An abyss of I'm-basically-doing-all-right-and-the-world's-treating-me-okay."

"And we're concerned about that little rant, are we not?"

"Yes, very." Two words but she speaks them with a quality halfway between briskness and effervescence, that was the best part of both, that reminded me of what I liked about Emily.

Porter takes longer to respond. But he knows this territory more deeply. "Yes, he's been journeying in his own head. He's been journeying without a god and without a friend. Nothing good will come of that." For all the melodrama of Porter's diction, this actually feels spot on.

Porter's insight into Serenity's pain feels like too much to consider right now, so we spend some time discussing the relative merits of *Seinfeld* and *Mad About You*. We decide that we relate to *Seinfeld*, which Emily calls "an ode to the wisecrack lifestyle." *Seinfeld*, God bless it, made friendship and irony seem like a plausible foundation for something like happiness. But we aspire to *Mad About You*, because the characters had found love and that was kind of the point.

Having arrived at another uncomfortable conclusion, Emily lights and rapidly burns down a cigarette. We finish our coffees, button our jackets, and disband, to be alone in our own thoughts, a little less Godless and friendless than we would be without each other, without this talk, without these wisecracks.

As I am walking back home, Emily catches up to me, even though her route home is in the opposite direction on Grand Avenue. She is breathless.

"I'm sorry. God, I'm in horrible shape," she wheezes.

"No problem," I say, a little baffled.

"I just wanted to say, I was sorry for, um, some of the things I said to you Friday."

"Oh, no, that's okay," I assure her. I am lying, though. It wasn't okay.

"I thought I could have phrased things better," she says.

"Well, thank you," I say.

"Oh, God, I hope I didn't just make it worse by talking about it."

"Or by talking about talking about it."

"Jeez."

"No, sorry, just kidding," I say, hating myself for making her feel worse. "I really appreciate the gesture."

"OK, thanks," she says, stopping as I keep walking.

I turn back. "No problem. See you next week."

"Yes, thanks." She says with a surprising vulnerability.

"Seriously, no problem," I say.

"Do you still not have gloves?" she asks, looking at my hands.

"No," I say. "But I do have pockets."

Are we bullshitters? Maybe. And yet we do these crazy little apologies, like the one Emily just attempted, which we never would have attempted before and a person who does something like that isn't entirely about telling themselves that everything is okay. I'm not sure what Emily was trying to do, but it had to do with some bigger shift in the self.

And the alloy of delusion and truth that we say to each other in group primes you for private insight. This morning's insight came randomly, as I was walking to what passes for home.

2

As I approach Dunn Brothers for the second time that wet December day, this time in the evening, driving my BMW, I envy the time I'd seen Franny walk past the downtown Minneapolis restaurant all that time ago and I ran out, leaving Pooch Labrador at the table, and blurted out what I felt.

I've had too much time to think about this encounter. I tell myself, repeatedly, "Make this about her, make this about her, make this about her." After working with Serenity, I've found that tense situations are far less anxious when I focus on what the other participants need. I am getting more cunning about my self-interest.

Of course, Dunn Brothers is as crowded as a physics blackboard. After making my way to her through the populated tables, hugging her as quickly as possible because someone was hovering right behind me with lattes in both fists, and exchanging hopeful "hey there's" that sounded straight out of high school, I say, "It was so great to see you yesterday."

"It was nice to see you too."

(I said "great." She said "nice." Let's set that aside.)

I won't twice forget to ask this: "But I was too dazzled by all the cereal to ask how you've been."

She laughs and says, "You would be dazzled by cereal."

Then she considers her answer to my question. "How am I? I was going to say 'fine' or 'good' or one of the tepid things you always say because, you know, who could stand a world where we all went around saying how we actually were doing?"

I think of how Porter, Emily and I might riff on that statement, improvising disturbingly precise spiritual weather reports.

"But you deserve a better answer than that."

"Hit me with it," I say.

She looks to the side and into the distance, not considering my face.

"I don't think I was wrong to do what I did," she says.

"No, I don't think you were," I say, although I don't quite believe it.

"What?" she asks. The talk of the rush hour crowd overlaps and amplifies itself, as people keep trying to talk over the general buzz.

"No, I don't think you were wrong" I say, almost shouting.

"Thank you," she pronounces. She leans in, her breath now warm on my ear. "The problem is, and I should probably hold this card closer to my chest, but the problem is, there have been so many things that I wanted to talk with you about—and not, like, state-of-the-relationship things but just daily things. You're the person I want to share the news of my day with."

She pauses and asks, "My question is, do you think you've changed? Because the person you were hurt me and I don't want to be hurt again."

Her face is serious; her arms, crossed in front of her sleek down coat, tightened, as if she is hugging herself for warmth.

How to sum up the wispy epiphanies of the past few months in a way that made sense to anyone? "Have I changed? I think so."

Her face hardens at this lame formulation. But she remains silent.

"And here's why I say that," I continue. "I was in a sort of group therapy meeting this morning."

"You're getting therapy?" she asks, brightening. "That's positive."

She wipes her face with the back of her hand.

"Oh, thanks. And yeah, I think it really has been. Our group leader who we call Sergeant Serenity . . ."

She says, "That's pretty good."

"Oh yeah, yeah it is." I want to tell Serenity stories but I don't.

"I was in a meeting this morning and people were talking about recent incidents that I knew about, incidents where I'd been there, and I realized that they were bullshitting themselves. They weren't lying precisely. But they were leaving things out and spinning other things in ways that made them look good. So that made me unsure if we ever see ourselves clearly."

"I think we see ourselves clearly enough," she says.

"Yeah, I agree," I say. "I think we can see ourselves clearly enough to grow."

She is silent.

"I mean," I start, "after the meeting I was walking home"—I don't mention my encounter with Emily—"and it occurred to me that I became a success before I became an adult."

Franny leans in. Her hands are close to mine. "That's pretty good," she says, "But what exactly does it mean?"

"I'm not exactly sure. I just liked the phrase."

"I think I know. I've been spending a lot of time thinking about what happened to us. I mean, my dating life since we broke up hasn't improved my opinion of men."

"Oh," I say, almost gasping. Then, hopefully, boyishly, fishing for an affirmation. "So you realized my awesomeness?"

"Duane," she says. "You hurt me. There's damage that will take a while to undo."

"I'm sorry," I say, because I want this so badly. But something in me resists it. Something in me suspects she's played the martyr and the manipulator. Something in me is just stubborn and childish about being judged at all, by anyone.

"Let me be clear," she emphasizes. "I'm here because I missed you. I'm here because you're the person I want to talk to at the end of the day. But I want to ask you two things: do you understand that you hurt me and what do you see in me?"

"Okay. Fair enough. Yes, I have hurt you." I feel the chill wind you feel when you see yourself clearly. I am almost sick to my stomach.

"And, what's the second question? That first one threw me."

"Why do you want to be with me? I don't want to be together out of inertia. I'd rather be alone, as dismal as that has been."

"I love that you are nice to the mentally challenged," I say. "I love that you have a bright clear laugh. I love that when we eat a meal made with saffron you think about whether the sailors who sailed from Portugal 500 years ago got a chance to taste the saffron. I love that you are deeper and better than me."

"Thank you. And I'm not better than you. I love that you are enthusiastic and passionate and that you love to make beautiful useful things. I love that you are fearless. I love your essential decency."

"Oh boy," I say.

"Indeed," she says.

We aren't quite sure what to do next.

I pivot, frantically. "So, really, how have you been?"

"Not great. Work's frustrating because the world sucks and evil wins." She means real evil, structural racism, structural poverty, not a client who doesn't like an idea.

She continues, "I had a whole thing with my mother, who thinks I'm a tramp."

"Really?"

"I told her I was protecting myself when we broke up."

"You were," I say, being slightly better than I am.

"Thanks, but I got pretty lonely. I mean, I suppose I shouldn't admit that, but one of the things about us is that we've never had to keep that kind of coy first-date distance."

"Yeah, we just liked each other."

"That whole having to be a showroom model of yourself so the other person doesn't think you're needy."

"There were all these things that I wanted to share with you. Like I said, you were the person I wanted to talk to at the end of the day."

She puts her hand forward on the table until it touches mine. "This is really public," she says.

"Yeah, where do you want to go?"

"My apartment."

As we stand up, she encloses my hands with hers. She looks into my eyes. A covenant of some sort is sealed. Someone behind me harrumphs judgmentally and asks if he could have our table. We leave. I really wanted her now, in that same dizzying way I had wanted her on the bus.

3

The sex is over quickly, which I'm not happy with myself for. But I suspect it isn't really over. We stay there, wide awake, naked, embracing and talking, staring or pausing and then, as we begin to negotiate, separating.

"I know it sounds stupid but I think you're my soulmate," I say.

"No, it doesn't," she says.

"I think I need to stop thinking every argument about a headline or a photo shoot is the end of the world." I am about 90% sincere and about 10% dishonest. I exaggerate my self-criticism, beating myself up, for obscure reasons.

Or perhaps not so obscure reasons: I want her to correct me.

"Sure, but that's not what I'm asking, honey."

"I'm sorry," I say. "I didn't quite say what I meant. I know what being a grown-up looks like. I just can't describe it."

She waits for me to try, rubbing the back of her neck. She's had a long day.

I say, "I don't think I'm going to work it out here. I think it has something to do with acknowledging that everybody cares, which is good, and that everybody has their own sensibility and agenda and that I'm not a god, despite the evidence to the contrary."

She laughs.

I continue, "I'm only half kidding. I really believe that I am always right, that at least when it comes to questions of design, God and I are peers, and these lesser, kind of annoying beings should really snap to."

"Yeah, maybe dial that down. But don't give up your standards. I don't want a husband who doesn't care about his job."

As soon as I hear "husband" I move closer to her again. This time the sex is better.

She falls asleep before I do and, as I lay there in the dark, I wonder if the higher power which I collage out of walking and service and meditation and exercise and prayer and talk with friends and talk in rooms where people imperceptibly change and, most recently, the love of the woman who is sleeping beside me would be up for the task at hand.

I look at Franny and I hope—hope that I won't sabotage what we'd just glued back together, hope that the qualification and stubbornness that tickle in my mind won't regather strength.

EMILY

That little apology to Duane was a test or what in the real world passes for a test because there was no clarifying grade scrawled in red on my Lawrence Durrell paper but only my vague sense, after sorting through the even vaguer variables and incomplete information, of what exactly happened. That was a test of *Can I relate to a man as a human being and not as an addictive substance/convenient tool?* This was a test of *Can the drama be dialed down to Everyday or Functional or Non-Cataclysmic?* This was a test of *Can I be nice?* I think I passed.

And I think Duane understood what I was trying to do. For all his boyish roller skating through life, Duane is not entirely without insight. I'm trying to be a different person.

PORTER

At the pet store, I pick a bag of treats from the many choices I have in this supermarket for pets, this shrine to Saint Francis's love. When they ask me what kind of dog I have, the question surprises me. I say, "I have a greyhound named Caper."

"Oh that's funny. There are people who come in here regularly who have a greyhound named Caper. A beautiful tawny girl. What a coincidence."

I redden, I hope, imperceptibly. "Yes, it certainly is," I say. But I drop the bills out of my wallet, bills which seem dirty in ways in which the currency of respectable people is not. They flutter to the floor.

"I'm so sorry," I say, placing them on the counter.

"No need to be sorry," the young woman at the counter says. But I see a flicker of concern in her eyes and hear it in her voice. I know that I look like a mug shot: wild gray hair, bald spot, thrift store clothes, the decaying tennis shoes she can glimpse as I exit the store.

Human Interaction 101

1

The alarm dredges me out of sleep, in its apocalyptic way. Franny's bare back moves toward the alarm; she tells it to shut up and smacks it silent.

We've shared the covers without too much violence or inequity. When she tugged in the night, I'd been careful to let her spool them to her.

She raises herself on her elbows, and says, "Wow. So here we are." We kiss, with almost closed mouths, so as not to inflict our morning breath on each other.

"So here we are indeed," I say.

Her expression is in the wry, bemused quadrant. She is naked except for the sea-foam green striped covers she clung to her.

I sit up and look around; she leans into me, warmly. The room gives off a Martha Stewart vibe—distressed armoire, white wainscoting, oxidized metal vases. On the wall, a looming Magritte apple and a sophisticatedly childish illustration of a woman which I would not otherwise like, because it feels too vulnerable for something designed and printed. These posters feel like people I'd once spent a very happy weekend with. Her familiars. My familiars. I spot the modernistic bamboo Quonset hut of a jewelry case I'd bought her, the mirror with a copper frame bordered with gold birds she inherited from her grandmother. And I notice what is unfamiliar: a new berry-colored candle.

"Secret Santa gift," she says, nodding at the candle.

Next to the candle are matches from Khyber Pass, a restaurant we wanted to visit but hadn't; and a Christmas card she'd brought into her bedroom.

A furnace rumbles. Her apartment is an old place with floral metal vents.

She puts her arm around me. It is pleasantly warm. We are all furnaces. "I so want to stay here but it's Tuesday and I gotta fly."

"Of course." I've forgotten the minor intensities of the workday morning. I've always loved those intensities—the fuel of coffee, the anticipation of work. But my rush hour muscles have atrophied. I want to sink back to sleep.

"I'm going to shower first, if that's okay," she asks.

"I've got no place I need to be," I say and wish I hadn't.

"Sorry," she says. "I know we may need to talk more, but I gotta fly."

"Go, fly," I say, with what I hoped was jauntiness.

"OK. Cool," she says, then hesitates, then says, "Do you need to pee or anything?"

"No, I'm good."

"Cool," she says, shedding the sheet and leaving, sheepishly, for the bathroom.

"Holy buckets, it's cold," she says, from the hallway. I keep a blanket wrapped around me and fight sleep.

I hear the fan start, the faucet run, the shower surge. Assured that she's occupied, I approach the Christmas card on her bureau: a tasteful picture of Central Park covered in snow. I lift the corner up and discover a letter inside, reading what looks like "Keith Arundel" on the return address. I start to open the folded letter but think better of it. The shower continues. I continue to not read the card.

Finally, I pull on my clothes.

"I see you're getting Christmas cards," I say, when she returns.

"Yeah, it was from a high school friend. He was making amends."

"Oh, that's good," I say.

"Yeah, sweet guy but messed up. We never connected."

"Hmmm," I say.

"You've got nothing to worry about. He's married and he lives in Baltimore. And he's probably still messed up."

"Sorry to be insecure," I say. "I know it's not very sexy."

"It's sexy enough," she says, and starts pulling on her clothes, but then walks toward me. We hold each other lightly, and then not lightly. I think of the Peter Gabriel song "In Your Eyes." The resolution of all my fruitless searches. Really? A pop song? Yes.

"Okay," I say, finally. "You need to get to work. I don't want to slow you up. I should pee and flee." It is a phrase we'd cooked up when we lived together. It makes her smile as she buttons her blouse.

I start to walk around her, but then turn and hug her one last time. She hugs me back; I rest my chin on her head; and she presses her face into my chest. She smells of expensive gentle shampoo and the air feels pleasantly warm and humid and I'd earlier noticed that the bedroom smelled of talcum and the bathroom smelled of potpourri.

"I'm so glad we're back," I say.

"So am I," she says.

"I'll call you tonight."

"Cool," she says. "And don't think I'm not a little sorry about how I acted when I broke us off."

I hadn't expected this, given her tone last night. "Thank you," I say.

She says, lingering, "You know why I couldn't lead with that?"

"Yes, I do," I say and I think I mean it.

As I leave the duplex a few minutes later, I feel the oddest mix of joy and fear. And I do have something to do today: I am having lunch with Pooch Labrador.

2

The last time I drove to Minneapolis was when I drove into work on my last day at the agency. But now I'm meeting Pooch Labrador for lunch at an almost-Cuban place called Chez Bananas. Etch A Sketches, crayons, and white butcher paper adorn every table. So every table is a potential art project. If all this stuff is a gimmick, as hipper souls insist, I realize I love gimmicks. I also know that other advertising people love gimmicks, too—we monetize gimmicks—so I'm afraid of meeting someone I know from the business. We are only a few blocks from my old firm.

I've known Pooch since high school. I trust him.

But I am still job-interview nervous, even though I am months away from being able to work again. I know enough about how things happen that I know that every interaction matters, that my stock can rise or fall, that sequences of events might be initiated or halted, that conversations could be sparked or shaped. I want whatever opportunity might flow from this lunch, I want to return to what we called "the business." I've always wanted this. I want to make elegant things that help ideas become money and money become prosperity and prosperity become ideas and ideas become things.

By elegant, I mean both surprising and efficient.

By things, I mean ads and posters and billboards and television commercials.

By money, I mean money.

By prosperity, I mean the generosity my mother extended to me and which I have extended to no one. By prosperity I mean, I will always have food, I will always have shelter, I will always have art supplies. I will always be able to make things and thus feel like a useful human and not an ambulatory cloud of neuroses.

No, that is not quite honest. I also want (very, very much want) to glibly offer my credit card as I pay for the brands I love a little too much. I want to buy Ralph Lauren crew socks and Brooks Brothers shirts and tickets to a Cowboy Junkies show or a jaunt to Chicago for a weekend. Although my partners are paying me a generous settlement, I can see the end of that stream, so I'm shaving with Barbasol, which I tell myself is what my father used without a single complaint. And yet I visualize going to the Clinique counter at Dayton's and buying glossy and luxurious shaving cream in tubes of restrained gray with sans serif type. I am betting that Pooch will expense this lunch.

I've grown used to the village pace of Grand Avenue. Minneapolis strives and strides and shines. It is a place of granite and glass skyscrapers—that wheat and water skyline—and aggressively reclaimed warehouses. Fortunately, when I enter the restaurant, a red brick place with lots of windows, I recognize Pooch and no one else.

With his pinpoint shirt and repp-stripe bow tie, his firm handshake and sincere smile, he counteracts my recent ethereal sadnesses. Pooch is Monday—the good parts of Monday, the parts that rinse away Sunday—as a person. "Good to see you, sir," he says, getting up from the table, and shaking my hand.

"What's new?" I ask.

I've only been out of the business for six months but Pooch answers, "A lot."

"Should I start with email or the world wide web?" he asks. "Or the crazy new designs?"

"I know a little bit about email, so let's start there," I say. I don't mention my knowledge comes from the new mom from group. Perhaps best not to mention group.

"Well, we can now all send each other messages through our computers. I haven't seen a pink "While You Were Out" slip in a month."

"Okay," I say. "That seems sensible."

"Everyone's so jazzed up about it, sensible is kind of beside the point. But, yeah, it is. But I find myself getting into fights unlike anything an old-fashioned memo ever provoked."

"That's weird."

"Tell me about it, but it happens. It has something to do with losing the human voice and, I think, the human face."

"You're not a guy who gets into fights."

"I'm not normally a guy who thinks about the human voice."

"True."

"But, yeah, I've gotten into a few email fights and they felt awful."

The waitress appears.

Pooch says to her, "I have to say, the Etch A Sketch is kind of genius."

"Have you tried it yet?" she asks.

"This is who should try it," he says and points to me. "Absolutely brilliant art director."

"Thanks for keeping expectations low," I say, but she's already hustling back to the kitchen with our order.

If this is an ur-pre-quasi-job interview, it is a fiendish one. I pick up the red plastic screen and manipulate the knobs. Chaos. I shake the Etch A Sketch to clear it. My failure to work this child's toy irritates me.

"You know, the whole point of being an art director is that you *direct* the art," I say, trying to keep my tone light. "You don't actually do anything."

"Sorry, man. Didn't mean to put you on the spot."

"Give me a second here," I say. "I think I have a concept."

"I knew you would," he says.

"We'll see about that," I say, perspiration starting to form beneath my arms. As I twist the knobs, I realize that it really is like riding a bike: a childhood skill that at first seemed impossible to your mind but then felt familiar to your muscles.

Realizing a visual concept with two knobs and a gray-on-gray screen isn't easy. You can't lift the pen off the page. You can't erase mistakes, except by starting over. I've evidently thought a lot about this particular technology.

Fortunately, the Chez Bananas logo can be rendered as a single line. I swear I stick my tongue out while I work.

I turn the little machine toward Pooch.

"You drew their logo? Cool."

"Everyone loves pictures of their kids. Everyone loves the sound of their own name. The reason why clients always want their logo bigger is because they love their company."

"You believe that last bit?"

"I've decided to start giving clients the benefit of the doubt."

"That's awfully grown-up of you."

"I've had some time to think about things."

"I bet," he says. "You shouldn't be sidelined like this," he says. "We need you in the business." He looks like he is considering saying more, but then he flags down the waitress and says, "You have to see what my friend did."

She is impressed, I think.

3

"It's a new world," Pooch is saying. "Besides the web sites, there's this crazy new design."

"That sounds okay. I liked how we've gone away from the same big sans serif headlines and ironic stock photos in the past few years. All that '80s stuff was starting to feel stale." It's nice to talk to someone who understands what I was talking about. Even though Pooch wasn't what we called a "creative"—a writer or art director or one of the creative directors, picked from their ranks, who led them—he is in advertising because he loves being close to the headlines and the layouts and the photo shoots.

"You wouldn't recognize this stuff," he says. There's a tone I'd never heard in his voice before: the kind of contempt you hear in small towns, fear that thinks it's something better than fear, fear that thinks it's common sense, fear that doesn't know it's hate. "It's very punk rock."

"Really," I say, and can't imagine what he's talking about—I can't imagine actual punk rock being applied to art direction. I suspect he wasn't using the term in the most rigorous possible way.

"Would they have it at the Walker?" I ask.

"The Walker is the mothership," he says.

After lunch, I drive down Hennepin, pivoting at Loring Park where Hennepin became generous and pastoral, Loring Park on one side, the sculpture garden brightened by the cherry spoon on the other. I head south to the squat, brick-and-glass modern building that houses the Walker and the Guthrie Theater. The Guthrie side is elegant with glass, but the Walker side struck me as oddly piled, distinct, almost free-standing blocks.

Inside, I understand the purpose of those blocks: containment and definition: impossibly clean, white walls, boring and bright as heaven: the most vigorous frames ever. Ever since I first stepped into this place, as an 18-year-old, shaken by driving the city freeways for the first time, these galleries were what possibility looked like. This is why humans invented cleaning: to achieve this purity, to allow things to become suns.

On that first visit to the Walker, a two-hour drive to a place I did not yet know, my first lone visit to a city of any kind, lost, rattled by traffic, honked at by a man with the fat face and violent eyes of a Quinn Martin police commissioner, not knowing if I was in the right neighborhood, stopping at a Burger King somewhere (where?) and asking for directions, speaking for the first time to Black people (they pointed me in the right direction) so I could stand next to artwork even Mr. Gould dismissed with a complacent smirk, I was surprised when I stepped inside and saw someone I knew, someone a few years older than me, the brother of our class president. He was someone who had spoken softly, who was better friends with the girls than with the boys, and who had gone to Harvard in part to escape the snickering and silence of the Minnisapa nice guys and, I presume, the cruelties of the not-so-nice Minnisapa guys. He was spending the summer in Minneapolis, interning somewhere, and, on that particular afternoon, attending a play at the Guthrie, which shared a lobby with the Walker Art Center. We'd greeted each other warmly, two Minnisapa strays, and, before he disappeared into the audience for some 18th century comedy, we'd had the easy conversation that the striving accomplished young have.

On this winter day more than fifteen years later, I find the magazines Pooch mentioned in the bookstore.

He wasn't kidding about the new style: it is punk as applied to graphic design: neon green type, gap-toothed kerning, *R AYGU N*, (a comma in the masthead), line spacing that harasses the line beneath it, hipster musicians with their eyes covered by sunglasses and their midriffs exposed, broth-colored light; no, urine-colored light. Then there is *Emigre*. A dark red cover, possibly mocking the term "full bleed," a black mass of ink in the shape of what looks like a fedora or an anvil with a caliper dangling from it, the words "Broad" in outlined cartoony type and, below that, the word "Cast" in another outlined cartoony font filled in with pink.

God has given the world an assignment: Tell Duane that every feeble assurance he's grasped for in design, every escape from human messiness, every deceitful moment of purification and control that he's ever indulged in has been ripped from him.

Well, fuck you, world. Kern this.

Later that afternoon, when I drive the keyline of my holiday card to the printer, passing the diners and bars and storefront churches and indifferent steak houses of University Avenue, I think about the designs I'd seen at the Walker. I can't quite bring myself to like them—liking needs to be effortless, what you feel for Sports Center or Neapolitan ice cream or a cute woman in a blue anorak/pea coat. But I do feel the beginning of admiration. Admiration can be negotiated and achieved. Especially as I studied *Emigre* a little more, there was something in its incisions and muddinesses and asymmetries and dissonances that felt like the designer had included parts of himself that had been edited out of more streamlined designs. Not quite grief—after feeling the shock of the new, I sensed something both comic and classic in the layouts; with a little more time, I could feel the grids which the designs carefully transgressed—but *something*.

The printer lifts the flap, checks to see if everything is in order, reads out, silently, to himself, "'Nothing is perfect except the light falling on imperfection,'" smiles wistfully, and says, "True enough, brother."

4

On Wednesday, I wake to the spare, introspective life I'd grown accustomed to. But at 9:30 I receive a call. It's Pooch Labrador.

"Do you think you could come in and talk to our Creative Director between Christmas and New Year's?"

"But I've got a non-compete," I say, flustered, never having even hoped for something this quickly.

"Things might be negotiable," Pooch says.

"Awesome," I exclaim. Easier said than done, I think.

"I do want you to know that you'll be coming in at one level below where you were. You'd be a senior art director, not a partner, and you'd report to Greg Bryant." Bryant had been at MegaMeta before I got there. I don't know him but I knew his brand: He is, vaguely, one of us in that he views a good headline and a smart layout as a moral achievement. He is neither a sellout nor a prima donna. Family man. Suburban. B+ talent, A+ personality.

"That still sounds awesome," I say, with too much adamance.

"Cool," he says.

With that, a feeling of exhilaration and fear enters me with such vehemence I checked to see if the windows are open. They aren't.

Franny had told me to stop by around six. I knock, let myself in, and find her holding her head in her hands at the kitchen table. She looks tired and discouraged.

"Oh hi," she says, looking up.

"How are you?"

"Kinda horrible," she says. "One of our clients is going to have to spend Christmas in jail."

"Can I do anything to help?"

"Pass the bar, become a judge, and take on this case."

"If I could, I would," I say.

"I know you would," she says. "It's just that the judge is being a prick, and I got the wrong lawyer for this one. If I'd been a little smarter, we would have gotten a buddy of the judge to take this. I just didn't think this through."

"You're not stupid."

"I am, but thanks for saying that. Now, this kid's mom is going to have to bring him his presents and fruitcake in jail."

Silence.

"It wouldn't be so bad if he'd done it, but it looks like he didn't."

Silence.

"I'm worse than Scrooge. I screwed up Christmas more."

"Scrooge didn't care. You did."

"Scrooge came around. This, on the other hand, isn't going to change," she said.

EMILY

I'm walking to Dunn Brothers with Porter. "I don't know," I say. "I feel like I'm a freshman in the school of life and I'm taking Human Interaction 101."

"That's pretty much the definition of the human condition. You're doing fine."

We walk down this street of spiritual immigrants: farm kids from the outstate who craved the city, people who've come to Minnesota from the coasts for official rehab and are now working sobriety jobs in coffee shops or hipster boutiques, people like me and Porter who just wound up here. "I'm thinking of hosting a party and I'm close to losing my mind."

"No, parties are good."

"I don't know," I say, "It's people in a room. Too many variables. Too many subtleties. Too much inflection and combustion. Too much history."

"That's an argument against all human interaction," Porter says.

"Precisely," I say. Porter chortles. There's a blast of December air and we both hug our coats closer.

"Cool. You chortled."

"Is that good?"

"Yeah," I thought it only happened in books. It's a short coughlike laugh. Deeper than a chuckle, less deep than a guffaw."

"So it is."

"Actually, I have no idea what a chortle is. That's just what I think it is."

"Good enough."

We examine the eclairs and danishes and scones as if they were diamonds and we were billionaires.

PORTER

I ask, "I am invited to your party, right?"

"Of course, you're invited," she says.

My soul dances. Then my old friend, shame washes over me. *I've extinguished souls. I don't deserve parties. I deserve to be a man who eats dinner from cans and loses himself in grainy reruns and dreams of gentle dogs.*

"Come back to me, Porter," Emily says. "Come back to me, friend."

I do.

Holiday Music and the Smell of Baking

1

I like Christmas shopping more than I should, given the bad rap that commercialism and materialism have received. Of course, I'm all about commercialism and materialism.

I will spend today pleasantly alone, moving through a holiday world (except that Franny might stop over and say goodbye which might mean having sex before she leaves for Alexandria).

I will spend the day floating in the river of shoppers and clerks and Christmas flaneurs, among the holiday music and the smell of baking, and passing the cheerful flotsam of evergreens and colored bulbs, running generous and thus spiritualized errands.

I will spend the day with the admittedly tenuous, persistently flickering possibility of employment and the reality of love and friendship.

I start with coffee and a white chocolate raspberry scone from a place on my block called Bread and Chocolate and a stroll through a cooking implement store called Cooks which makes me happy, even though I don't really cook, because it is all chrome and Bakelite and new books and porcelain on blonde hardwood floors and blonde hardwood displays. Outside, they were roasting chestnuts over an open fire, for chrissakes.

I then get into my car and drive to the REI on the almost-bohemian West Bank, with its dive bars and grad students and organic restaurants and communist bookstores. I buy Trevor his Swiss army jackknife and then I'm off to the St Paul Dayton's to buy Jenny her ear muffs (I wanted to say hi to Emily but she wasn't working) and then back to Grand Avenue, to Wet Paint to buy my niece and nephew their art supplies. After some consultation about what was age-appropriate—twenty-dollar Swiss drawing pencils would be lost on them—I find some jacked-up crayons and nice sketchbooks and watercolors they probably wouldn't find in Minnisapa.

This leaves my gifts for Franny.

And once I focus on this, things get complicated. For all my kind of stupid enthusiasm for Christmas, I know at least one emotional truth: gifts are complicated. Gifts crystallize listening. Gifts show you've been paying attention. Gifts calibrate relationships. I know this because Franny has explained it to me. Her parents prepared her for parts of life that mine never paid any attention to. Some might say they prepared her for the more shallow parts of life, but I don't think so. Her father had the social and political skills you need to arrive as a New York Italian in a Scandinavian central Minnesota town and succeed. Her mother—the daughter of prosperous farmers—grew up watching Grace Kelly and Katherine Hepburn movies as life instruction manuals and convincing herself that she'd been raised on the Philadelphia main line.

Of course, this history suggests my gift to Franny: I will find some DVDs of Grace Kelly and Katherine Hepburn movies. I visit the video store on Grand but find only beat up rental copies, and so I drive to the damn mall and buy them at a Best Buy where someone steals my parking space, sending my blood pressure up. I grab *Bringing Up Baby* and *The Philadelphia Story* before someone who is babbling about "a family Christmas with their kids" got them, sending their blood pressure up, and the clerk groaned at my perhaps too-detailed explanation of the awesomeness of this present before wishing me a Merry Christmas. Everyone sent everyone else's blood pressure up, and it was a fine Christmas moment.

"Want them wrapped, sir?"

"I'd kick your ass in wrapping."

"I'm sure you would."

"No, I meant that to be funny."

"Have a Merry Christmas, sir."

I navigate back through traffic which feels newly committed to hindering if not threatening me and a poisonous drizzle which clearly does not have my best interests in mind. Wiser for my journey, I arrive at the Bibelot on gentle Grand Avenue and buy a lovely silver alpaca shawl, because I want to buy something that will touch her skin. And because I've forgotten her size.

Franny stops by at 5:30, bundled in a parka and scarf, and carefully carrying a wrapped rectangle. She looks happy.

"Hey, how you doing?" she asks.

"Not bad," I say, simplifying the day for the good of everyone concerned.

"Merry Christmas!" she says.

"Come in," I say. "Do you want anything?"

"Several of those," she says and points to the scones I'd bought at Bread and Chocolate. "And maybe some coffee? I'm beat, and I still have to drive to Alexandria tonight."

"Really, you can't hang out?"

"Maybe a little," she says.

I grind coffee.

"Oh, that smells wonderful," she says.

"Thanks," I say. "I've got a few presents for you."

"And I've got this for you." She shakes the package lightly. "I'm kind of psyched to give it to you. But I'm afraid because you might hate it and feel compelled to keep it. You'll see."

It is artwork. Nothing else is that flat and that square. Subjectivity on a stick. I might wind up with something I don't care for on my walls. "I'm sure I'll love it and I'm pretty happy with what I got you."

"Cool. I like having a boyfriend."

I start the coffee and grab her gifts from where a Christmas tree would be. "If yours is super cool, I want to go first because mine's pretty good but yours might be better."

"It's not a contest, honey."

"You sure?"

"Okay maybe it's a little bit of a contest."

"Hah," I say, half laughing, half proclaiming victory.

"But we can both win," she says.

"Sounds good," I say.

"Let's get this screwball comedy moving along here," she says.

"That's ironic," I say, thinking of her gifts.

"Really?"

"Never mind," I say.

"Okay," she says. "Here's mine for you. And remember, no matter what happens, we love each other."

"Um, sure. What's going to happen?"

"Open it."

I begin to carefully remove the tape.

"Faster," she says.

"I'm almost done," I say, revealing the corner of what she has found for me: an original painting by my high school art teacher Herb Gould, of a valley by New Luxembourg, in winter, with a stream and birches; it's painted with a delicate touch that makes it breathe in ways that 99.9% of the calcified conventional paintings you see in gift shops don't.

"Oh my God," I say. "Thank you so much."

"I'm so glad you like it!"

"I love it! Where did you find it?"

"Your friend Chimes Sanborn helped me find it. I called that bowling alley he runs because I couldn't quite remember your teacher's name and he pointed me to a gallery in White Bear Lake and I picked it up over my lunch hour."

"Oh, man," I say. "Here's yours. It's not as cool."

"It's really not a competition, honey."

I back away and pour her coffee, nervously watching, fine-tuning the cream, while she opens the shawl.

"Oh my God, this is lovely," she says. She hugs it to herself and feels the cloth. "This is exquisite," she says.

She opens the movies and begins to cry. "Oh my God, Mom's movies," she says.

"Happy tears? Sad tears?" I ask.

"Kinda both," she says. "Sadness because, when she was young before she learned to modulate things, those movies separated her from the good country people around her, who thought she was uppity, and that separation almost killed her, and then happiness because those movies made her who she was and then sadness because I, when I was younger, I rejected them in such a mean adolescent way—God, teenagers are sociopaths—and that hurt her and then happiness because we eventually bonded over them and now I love them. So, you know, kinda both."

We kiss and then we have sex on my futon and then she finishes her coffee, which I warmed up, and a scone and, once again, for us, coffee and pastries are afterplay.

"Do you still have the white tray we used to use?" she asks.

"I do."

"I love that stupid tray," she says.

"Me too."

She gathers her gifts. "Sorry to have my way with you and run but I really do have to get to Alexandria tonight and it's a long drive."

"I know. Thanks for stopping and thanks for the best gift ever."

"Goodbye," she says.

"Godspeed," I say, which makes her raise her eyebrows.

"No, I mean it. Drive safe," and we kiss goodbye and I realize that being in love means that when someone you care about is driving through the December night you worry.

"Call me when you get there," I say. "Here's the number at my sister's." I hand it to her.

"I will," she says.

EMILY

"Duane?" I say. "This is Emily, from group."

I am feeling *problematic*, at once too present, ethereal and frantic, like a fire or a tornado, and about to make a decision to not be there at all, drifting to the safety of the ceiling and looking down on this farce. I know we're all supposed to yearn to be "in the moment." Have you been in many actual moments? They're not pleasant.

"Of course," he says, like a person who does not think this present moment is a crisis.

And then, deftly ignoring my combusting, meteorological self, I say, "I was hoping to have a little holiday get together and I was hoping you could attend."

"I think so. When?"

I regroup and recalibrate, surprised at my little success. My mind and my body reunify, like old friends. "Monday at, let's say, seven. There will be food."

"Sure," he says, "Should I bring anything?"

"No, just yourself," I say.

"Cool," he says.

"No wait, why don't you bring whatever you want to drink?"

"I can do that."

"I'm going to get some food," I say then realize I've already said that.

"Good. I like food."

"Stop being a wiseass. This is the first time I've ever thrown a party."

"Good for you," he says.

"Sure," I say.

"I meant that, Emily."

"Thanks," I manage.

"I'm also going to bring little presents for everyone," he says.

"It's going to be me, you, Porter, Trevor, and Jenny."

"Cool. We can play pin the tail on the neurotic."

"That'd be me," I say.

"That'd be all of us," he says.

"It'll be great," he continues. "The first holiday party was in a manger and that went okay."

"Whatever," I say.

"You know that was Mary's first party."

"And those three dudes crashed it."

"And those donkeys."

"And she couldn't get the venue she wanted."

"And she was popping out a kid."

"And Joseph was, you know, suspicious."

"This will be way better than that."

"Way better," I say. "Thanks for cheering me up." This time I mean it.

"No problem," he says, and I only hope that's true. I'm nothing if not problematic.

PORTER

I have the names of Caper's owners from the Humane Society. I have their number, because no one has called me since they called me. I dial *69 and leave a message. I would, on second thought, like to see Caper.

On Christmas Eve day, the man in the couple calls—his name is Kyle—and asks if I can meet him and his wife and Caper on Summit Avenue, near Hamline.

It's a nice neighborhood, a tree-lined snow-covered boulevard between mansion-bordered lanes of traffic. They must have money. I'm holding a treat because it would be too heart-breaking if Caper were indifferent.

When I see her, I am filled with a ticklish joy. She seems to recognize me and points toward the treat. I extend my hand, and she nuzzles it. She's wearing a red jacket that makes her seem like a Christmas gift.

We walk. Kyle hands me the leash. Caper is curious and brisk and light on her feet.

"We were so glad you found Caper and took care of her. That was the worst night of our lives," he says.

His wife, Amanda, lifts her eyebrows.

"No, it wasn't the worst night of our lives. But it was a feeling I never want to have again."

"It was actually a magical night for me. This creature just appeared, and I was able to help."

"Caper's developed a taste for pizza," the wife says. "We're not sure how we feel about that."

"So, you deliver pizzas," the husband says. "Do you like that?"

"Yes, I do. I've driven cab and I've been in the army," I say. "And delivering pizza is my favorite. People are almost always happy to get pizza." I don't tell him that it's the only job I've had where I haven't killed someone.

"I suppose they are," he says. "When were you in the army?"

"Late '60s. I did a tour."

"In Vietnam?" he asks.

"Yes," I say. I brace myself for the standard "thanks for your service" or "those were dark times" that seem to be the younger generation's only responses to the war.

"My big brother was in Vietnam," he says. "Actually, he, um, died there."

"I'm sorry," I say. "I lost a lot of brothers."

"*That* was the worst night of my life," he says.

Caper continues her nose-reconnaissance and then circles and slows.

"What are you looking at, Caper?" Amanda says. "That's it. Mark that snow. Good girl."

We're walking about a block from Snelling Avenue.

As we turn to go back, Kyle says, "You know, we know you love Caper and we think that maybe we get together every three or four months for a walk, if you'd like that."

"Yes, I'd like that very much."

"We can meet here," he says.

"You live nearby?" I ask, although I suspect they are being careful about not revealing exactly which house they live in. Most of the mansions here have been converted to condos.

"We live in Roseville but I come by here a few times a week, though."

"Great," I say. He doesn't live here, but in a pleasant but modest suburban neighborhood to the north. He goes to AA meetings in the house we are approaching. My guess is that, when he drank, he spent a lot of time in seedy bars, around men like me, men that reminded him of his dead brother. My guess is that Amanda did not know him when he drank and that she now, out of love, indulges him in his occasional nostalgia for the seedy and the seeking.

"Merry Christmas," they both say as they pause before leaving.

"Merry Christmas," I say, "to you and to Caper." It occurs to me I should have gotten her a toy.

My guess is that she has plenty. She smiles and pants and kind of tugs in my direction. Then she follows them to their car, through the snow, in her red jacket. She bounces a little.

"You will play a larger part in my life than I will play in yours," I want to say, but I don't say anything. Christmas has always involved visits from animals.

Festive Jails

1

It is dark by five. I drive through versions and variations of light—
the glares and vacancies of freeways, the gray of the railroad yards,
the muted exurbs, the cones of my headlights and the glow of my
dashboard on country highways, the reflected light of fields in snow,
the street lights and glowing decorations of towns, the moonlit river,
the matte bluffs, the spotlit nativity at St Agnes, and then the teardrop blue Christmas lights, inherited from my parents, that grace
the spruce tree outside my sister's. Inside, a multi-colored tree glitters
and shines. The kitchen welcomes in the way of farm kitchens. My
niece and nephew wait in the window, then run to the door as my
wheels crunch the gravel.

After the children stop mobbing me, my sister Angela says,
"Franny called. She arrived safe."

"Wonderful," I say.

"I thought you guys broke up."

"We did. We got back together."

"Good, I like her. I think she'll be a good influence."

"I need a good influence?"

"Yes."

I don't celebrate Christmas quite so much as I audit it, although "audit" seems off because I am immersed more fully than I am in my actual life as we swim through our rituals. First, we shared the Christmas eve meal of my people—ham, mashed potatoes with pools of melted butter, sweet potatoes glowing with sugar, dressing, and then the edible cartoons of cookies, with coffee for the adults, with milk for the kids. Then a ten p.m. mass, the kids nodding off, the church packed, the language that still trudges and bewitches like the old Latin, the priest saying something about the true nature of gifts, how they differ from, say, lottery winnings in that they are infused with the giver, and then back home and the groggy children each opening one of my gifts, a tradition created especially for me, perhaps by my sister the propagandist as an ad for life with kids. I'm not saying it's ineffective. I'm not saying one might not crave such a life.

EMILY

I'm working Christmas Eve at Dayton's, this town's proud old department store. There are worse places to be on Christmas. Carols play; the store looks swanky; as harried as they are, people make an effort to be nice. Dayton's reminds me of the department stores I knew in Seattle, a sustained happiness of color and texture and service so nice it made you feel princessy.

Because it's Christmas Eve, there are a lot of men, which is good, and, as a perfume spritzer, I'm idle, also good.

Still, my feet hurt.

A cute—no, confident—man, a few years younger than me solidifies out of the crowd, "Give me a spritz," he says.

"It's a woman's cologne," I say.

"I'm man enough," he says. "Hit me."

In my taxonomy of men, I place him: law student, does stand up comedy or thinks about it, admires George Plimpton slightly more than is strictly necessary. He probably rode his bike here. President of his high school class. They still talk about his graduation speech. It was *crazy*.

I spritz him.

"Nice, overtones of lavender and puppies."

"Right about the puppies," I say. "Wrong about the lavender."

"Damn," he says and sniffs his wrist again. "I love it."

"Have a merry Christmas," I say.

"Merry Christmas," he says. "I have six presents to buy in the next twenty minutes."

"Well, there are at least seven things in the store," I say.

"What I have going for me is low expectations," he says. "I'm the youngest son."

"I know one of those," I say.

"I buy everyone gloves or chocolates, and they're just glad I show up."

"You only have 18 minutes left," I say. "I'm looking out for you."

"Thank you," he says. "Have a Merry Christmas. You're wonderful."

He doesn't say, "lovely." Points for that.

"Have a Merry Christmas yourself," I say and he hurries off, with just one fond flirtatious look back.

I wish I trusted men enough to pursue this, as absurd as it is.

I wish I trusted myself enough to enjoy the moment for what it is.

Wait, something unfamiliar is happening. I am, for a moment, happy. I'm a pretty girl and I'm going to take my goddamn pretty girl perk.

I'm going to go home, open my presents from my family, call home and thank them, and fall dead asleep. And a few days later, I will throw a gracious party.

PORTER

It is Christmas Eve and I'm delivering pizzas. The few people who are outside are bearing gifts. I've volunteered for this. The deliveries are light; the tips are good; it is a way of being of service.

I deliver a sausage and mushroom with extra cheese to a small boxy apartment building, up near the freeway.

I'm buzzed in and descend the salty steps and stand in front of the door, examined by the peep hole. The door opens tentatively.

"Hello, Porter," says the man on the other side—beak nosed, thin haired, with an angular medium build, dressed in corduroy slacks and a wan cardigan over a collared shirt. He's a man about my age who will always dress like he's dressing for school. I recognize him from church. Even to my blunt nose, the apartment doesn't smell good. He lives with his mother. There is in one corner, a tabletop tree; beneath that, are old copies of *Sport* magazine. There's a baseball strategy game that I remembered coveting in my childhood on the tabletop. A choir struggles from the speakers of a television.

"Hello, Max," I say.

He'd greeted me a few moments ago, before I saw how he lived, but now he looks down and away. He had expected the pizza delivery guy to be anonymous.

He gets his wallet.

"No," I say, "This is on me."

"No, no," he says. His words fray and sputter; he's a man who fears he's broken yet another rule.

"It's Christmas, a time for gift giving."

"No, please." He holds a ten he's extracted from his wallet.

"No, I insist, brother."

He takes the pizza, whose heat I can feel on my fingers.

"Thanks, man. Merry Christmas."

"Merry Christmas to you," I say. "I'll see you tomorrow." I go back to my car, my route, and my night. I like to think that I have blessed him but our encounter began with shame and I don't know which won, the shame or the blessing.

Home from my shift, I insert the VHS tape of the only Christmas episode the Andy Griffith show ever produced. Andy and Barney open a card from the Hunaker Brothers, who are cheerfully reunited in the state prison. A vulture-faced local merchant hauls in a fresh-faced family man who made his own batch of liquor, demands the man's arrest, and won't be persuaded to show any mercy. Andy then arrests the man's family so they can be together at Christmas and the Griffiths bring their celebration to the jail. They laugh. They sing. The rich man connives to get himself arrested, and bestows gifts—baseball mitts, roller skates, dolls—from his store.

I cry, contemplating this world of charming misdemeanors, festive jails, and unambiguous redemption. I cry, contemplating this world where there is no abyss. I cry, and I pray.

Beveled Plastic Hospital Glasses

1

It's the Monday of the week after Christmas and I've driven through nearly empty gleaming downtown Minneapolis to meet with the Creative Director at Pooch's firm. I park on the street and wipe my hands. The mirrored walls of the building giddily reconstitute me.

My nervousness can't cancel the love I have always felt for places where things are created, for lit, populated, industrious places. I shoulder through a revolving door. I have unnecessarily complicated feelings about revolving doors. I like them, because they are all big city and technicolor movies, but I also question whether they ask more of us than a door should ask of us. There is all that timing and committing and then that odd enclosed dance and then being spat back out.

I set down my portfolio to sign the guest book; my life's work leans against my leg. The security guard shrugs at my signature, the elevator opens, closes around me, and breathily ascends several floors, and I face a glass-fronted office. A few employees move through, oblivious and earnest; they might as well be in an aquarium. I assume they are project managers; they have the look of people quietly fending off chaos with to-do lists. On the window beside the door are three names in a discrete sans serif font with an ampersand which, according to what passes for legend around here, changes color every year, like a corporate mood ring. Their logo is now a snooty green. Somebody wants to be a consultancy.

The receptionist, sitting beneath a display of Christmas cards from photographers and printers and color separators and clients, brightly asks, "How can I help you?"

I'm tempted to be glib or to make the question "how can I help you?" seem more profound than it was ever intended to be. But I resist the temptation and say, "I'm here to meet Greg Bryant."

"Wonderful. He'll be right with you."

I sit in an oversized olive chair daubed with teal and mauve and graffiti'd with doodles. I've looked at the *New Yorker* and wondered at the fashion ads—seemingly concept-free, unless pouting is a concept—and I'm wiping my nervous hands on my pants when Greg emerges. He also looks cheerful. He's wearing loafers, khakis, and a navy Ralph Lauren polo. I'm wearing Timberlands, khakis, and a Brooks Brothers oxford. Close enough.

"Good to see you, Duane," he says, as we walk toward his office. "I don't think we've met but we have mutual friends."

"Exactly," I say. I know his brand. That means he knows mine and it may not be good.

"Of course, Mr. Labrador has great things to say about you," he says, with perhaps just a trace of irony. "And I've seen some of your work from the past several years."

I'm trying to read his tone—or rather, the strategy behind his tone—and I can't. Is he excited to see me? Or is he being nice so he can let me down less painfully?

He has achieved a large corner cube, filled with markers and layouts and pictures of his wife and children. There's no forced wackiness. A Macintosh sits grumpily in one corner, but it looks like the real work happens on a drafting board.

A subordinate approaches, realizes Greg is with me, and shoots him a "can I talk with you soon?" look. Greg knew the small, strong satisfaction of having your opinion matter.

"Let's see what you have," he says, turning out toward me, away from his drawing board. I rest my open portfolio on my knees.

"Nice," he says, and I explain and flip the pages.

"Nice.

"Yes.

"Very good.

"I remember that," he says of something which appeared as a TV campaign. "Nice seeing the print pieces. You know I have always loved print. More disciplined."

I agree, because I actually agree and because that is what I am going to do today. Even with the agency at half strength during the holiday week, there is work going on around me, people marking up type and brainstorming headlines in side rooms and discussing schedules and routing color separations. The fact that the office is half-empty just highlights the particulars more: the flap of proofs, the squeak of marker, the collision of voices intersecting at an idea, the shish of a project manager's strides, the flutter of gossip and the lilt of war stories. I know these sounds.

We finish my portfolio, and he says, "The work's great. Let's talk about the last months."

Jesus. There will be an accounting and it will not end well, and I will never work again.

"The past months have been tough," I say. I add, "I love this business."

"I know," he says. "What happened to you happens to so many people. You get to a place where you're doing well, but you're just a little too cocky, you don't quite know what you've got, you think you're untouchable."

He is going to some remembered place and some remembered self, a self that I sense he has outgrown but never quite left behind.

"And the next thing you know you're the first to get laid off because you're single and too f-you by half and you realize how lucky you were when you were working and you realize that punk attitude that felt so smart and righteous really was just immaturity. Or maybe you just get tired of drinking scotch in your underwear."

I look at the pictures of the wife and the children and smart, slightly conservative layouts and the markers he has not quite given up for a Mac.

"Exactly," I say.

"Good," he says. "I just want to confirm that what we have open is a senior art director position."

"Cool," I say.

"A step down," he says, "from where you were."

"I understand, and I'm eager to get back to work."

"Good, I just didn't want there to be any ambiguity."

"I understand. And thank you."

"Don't thank me yet. The decision isn't final." I haven't meant to presume I have the job. I meant to thank him for being clear about the position, even at the cost of awkwardness.

"Of course."

"We hope to make the decision sooner rather than later."

"Thanks for considering me," I say.

"Thanks for coming in," he says in the purposely clipped tone of someone who realizes he is conducting a job interview. I sense he wants to say more about what we share—the love of ideas flurrying onto paper, the love of concepts buffed by revision, the love of commerce as a soft spiritual exercise which gets you off your couch and into the world. But instead he beckons to the subordinate who needed to speak with him earlier. The junior bounds up, holding a layout. I nod and let myself out.

As I'm coming out, I see my old partner Brian half-obscured by the revolving door. He has his portfolio.

We can't avoid each other. I step toward him and extend my hand. "Good to see you," I say.

He looks up sluggishly. "Oh, yes, Duane. Good to see you."

Neither of us is supposed to be here. I am not supposed to be working at all. Partners such as Brian do not interview with other firms.

"Interview upstairs?" I ask.

He winces. He looks tired. "Yes."

"Well, good luck with it," I say.

"Thank you," he says.

"You'll knock 'em dead," I say.

"Yeah," he says, not at all convincingly. He wants to say more. I wait.

"Don't tell anybody. Even my wife doesn't know."

"Of course, I won't. Of course."

"We gave it a hell of a try, didn't we?" he says.

"Yes, we did," I say. I hadn't realized: the firm is failing.

He begins to weep. I give him room.

When he is done, he says. "I'm sorry. It was a tough Christmas." His face is raw and wet.

"I bet," I say.

He composes himself. "How do I look?"

"Let's see if we can't get the security guard to let you use the bathroom on this floor to clean up."

"Thanks, man," he says. "We were partners." He says it joyously, and sadly, like a boxer in a black-and-white movie, reflecting on past glories.

"Yes, we were," I say.

When I ask the security guard if Brian can use the bathroom, he says, "You got it, brother." He says it like a man who knows a job interview can save your life.

2

I am snug in my apartment, with a phone that hadn't rung, with a job offer that hadn't been extended. It is six. It isn't going to ring.

But I do have a party I've promised to attend. Franny has to work late. I'll leave for the party before she gets home. I don't understand why parties are such a good thing in theory and such a chore in practice. I just want to spend a quiet evening, sitting here, staring at the phone which won't ring and regretting my life choices.

I gather the gifts I bought. I've changed up my strategies for Trevor and Jenny and Serenity. For Trevor, a Walker Art Center membership, on the theory that the kid's just started searching and he might as well search somewhere good; for Jenny, some fancy lavender soap from the Bibelot, because the new baby seemed to have put the fancy soap part of her life on hold; and, for Serenity, a bag of Mounds bars, a gift I am aggressively reconsidering.

As I approach Emily's, I see Porter is already there. I have second thoughts—no, fourth thoughts— about gifts, but I proceed. I want love to be reduced to the simplicity of objects. But I think of what Franny told me: that around every gift is a nimbus of obligation and expectation.

I will into being a simpler world, where gifts are gifts.
It's just cold enough that I'm bothered that I don't have gloves.

At the party, to break the silence, I say, "So this is going to be awkward."
"I'm sorry. I've never thrown a party. In case you couldn't tell."
I'd meant to lessen the tension by joking about it. I hadn't intended to insult.
"I was actually referring to the 'the rest of our time on earth.' The party looks fab. Look at that food! White chocolate, be my friend" I exclaim and scoot to get some. It's not a big apartment and more Virginia Woolf than I'd imagined. I keep forgetting that Emily has a degree in literature, because being a self-centered, socially awkward dick takes up so much of my time.

"'The rest of our time on earth'? Nice save," Emily says.
Porter says, "I assume that the afterlife is going to be awkward, too."
"Soooo," I say, assuming the persona of a recent arrival in heaven. "Sure beats hell."
"My party?"
"No, heaven. And your party. Both are way better than eternal torment."
I really need to shut up.
Porter says, nodding toward the CD player, "I'm one of the few people who can resist dancing to George Winston."
The doorbell rings. Emily moves to get it. We turn to greet whoever is arriving, in our ironic awkward way. It's Jenny.
The group mind that Emily, Porter and I share, the additional self that's smarter and funnier than any of us, has been dissipated.
"Hello, everyone," she says, with too much hope, with a sincerity which confirms my fears.
Porter whispers to me, "Everything up until now was amateur awkwardness."

He may or may not have spoken too loudly. Emily, emerging with Jenny from the bedroom, where the coats gather like some sort of flock, asks, "What?"

"Nothing," I say.

Porter blushes. This is more than embarrassing to him. This is an awareness of sin. This is a shame he thinks he deserves.

The doorbell rings again.

What fresh existential algebra has been unleashed, I wonder, but don't say because I don't want to make Jenny any more uncomfortable than she already is.

It's Trevor. He looks like he's been running; his clothes—an army jacket over a flannel shirt--are akimbo; his hair messed up; his skin whiter than usual, the skin of someone who just built a basement in his basement.

"Um," he says, catching his breath. "Have you guys had a chance to check your answering machines?"

We shake our heads no, then look toward Emily's machine, tucked away between her kitchen appliances, toward the back of the apartment. It's blinking. She presses a button.

"Hello," a wavery voice says. "This is Tim Griffin's sister. I wouldn't normally call you but Tim is in trouble, and I thought you'd want to know. Can you call me?" The voice on the machine gives a number. Emily dials it. We gather around her.

"Yes, this is Emily. One of Tim's clients. I was told to call this number."

She waits while someone is, presumably, summoned. She looks at us and shrugs.

"Hello."

"---."

"Yes."

"---."

"Yes, I understand.'

"___."

"That's horrible," she says.

We glance at each other and do our best to discern a conversation from one person's speech.

Emily grabs a notepad with her one free hand, sets it down, and mimes writing with a pen. Jenny extracts a pen from her purse.

"Yes.

"Yes, I understand. I'm ready."

She begins to write.

She turns and says, "Mr. Griffin drank a quart of Scotch and he's detoxing. His sister said he asked for us."

"Seriously?" I ask.

"Yes. Evidently, we're his support group," Emily says.

"Jesus," Porter says.

3

"I hate parking ramps," I say as we approach the ramp.

"I hate hospitals," Trevor, who is riding with me, says, and I ponder the difference between what I mean when I say, "hate," and what Trevor means. I mean "hate" in the sense of aesthetic annoyance and consumer anti-preference, the kind of "hate" experienced by those of us who spend too much time thinking about records and movies and comic books. Trevor means hate in a different sense. Trevor means, "I hate hospitals because they recall for me the days when I was watching my father die and the soul sickness I felt as I approached his room and the sadness I felt as I left it. I hate hospitals because they remind me of a hole which will never be filled."

As I slow the car to a stop, a machine spits out a magnetized ticket, a wooden arm lifts; with me anxiously at the wheel, my foot ready to brake, my eyes darting left and right, looking for slight movements or tentative brake lights, we circle tightly through parked cars and concrete poles. When we walk to the elevators, I realize once again that I need gloves. An elevator opens; we step in; it ascends and opens again; glass doors whisk open; a cursory receptionist points us in a vague direction; a lobby grins with ecumenical holiday lights; then more elevators and hallways arrow us toward our destination—a white bed with metal rails containing Serenity: a sharp-edged man now unrecognizably puffy, bruised, defeated, dazed, sentience reduced to bafflement and shame.

"Oh, Mr. Griffin," I hear Trevor say. I say nothing.

"I'm glad you're here," Serenity says, without raising his head. He swallows hard. "I'm ashamed for you to see me like this."

"No, it's fine," I say.

"I can see the looks on your faces," he says. "I can hear the pity in your voices."

"Would you like some water?" I ask.

He nods "yes" and his head sinks farther back into the bed.

I pull the paper wrapper off a bendy straw and hear Porter and Emily enter.

"Oh, Mr. Griffin!" exclaims Emily.

"Please stop exclaiming," Serenity says. He seems pissed, his anger sparked and pushed by shame.

"I'm sorry," says Emily.

Trevor has left the room.

Serenity sips water from a straw extending from the plastic glass. I wonder why the glass—or plastic, really—in hospital glasses is always beveled. "I'm sorry," Serenity says. "It's been a rough couple of days."

For grip, I conclude; bevels make glasses easier for the weakened and wounded to hold.

"What did my sister say?" Serenity asks.

"She said that you'd started drinking at her family's Christmas," Emily, smarting a little, answers. "That you had been obnoxious, that you walked out when she confronted you about it, that when she and her husband and a paramedic friend arrived at your home, you were not there, that you had disappeared for two days, and that you had driven your car off the side of the freeway, and were found staggering along the shoulder."

"That's accurate," he says and adds, "as far as I can tell."

"Do you want to talk about what happened?" Porter asks.

"I mistook a memory for an abyss, Porter," he says. "And I fell into it."

"I know. People like us, we do that," says Porter. I realize that, as Vietnam Vets, he and Porter have a special bond, one that goes deeper than 'I lost my job in advertising.'

Jenny walks in with Trevor. She tactfully doesn't exclaim. "Hello, sir," she says and grasps his hand.

Trevor had left the room to warn her.

"You've helped us all out of our personal abyss, sir," Trevor says. "How can we help you?"

"You can't. You're my clients," Serenity says, exhausted. "I shouldn't have asked my sister to call you."

"We're here now," Emily says. "We're the self that's bigger than the self," she says. The self that's bigger than the self—it was one of Serenity's phrases, a handhold on the wall of the abyss.

"Do you need to talk?" Jenny asks.

"No, but it would be nice if you would talk. How was everyone's holiday?"

Emily and I look at each other, as if to ask 'really?' but then we both realize that, if your Christmas had tangoed with insanity before landing you in a hospital bed, you might want some dispatches from the comparatively sane world.

I begin. "I may have a job."

"I planned a party."

"I made deliveries. It's an old Christmas tradition."

"My mom and I got along and I bought presents for everyone," Trevor says. "It's not a job but it's a step forward."

"When I was anticipating Christmas, all I could see was the stress of hauling a baby between three houses in the cold," Jenny says. "But it was actually quite nice. Babies can bring out the best in people."

Serenity's eyes flicker, as if to shut.

"How long have you been up?"

"Two days," he whispers. "Give or take."

"I'd like to suggest something," Porter says. "Can we pray? You've mentioned it, as a strategy. But we've never done it."

Serenity is almost too weak to speak. "We're a secular therapy group. It wouldn't be appropriate."

"I'm cool with it and I'm a heathen," Emily says.

Everyone else nods.

Porter grasps one of Serenity's hands and Jenny grasps the other. Trevor grasps Jenny's other hand and Emily grasps Porter's other hand. I grasp Emily's hand—it is cool and knuckled—and reach across the bed rails to grasp Trevor's; it is warmer and slightly moist. I squeeze both, establishing whatever circle we sought to establish.

"Cold hands," Emily says.

"Colder heart," I say. She laughs. Porter clears his throat.

"It is Christmas and let us rejoice with those who rejoice," he says and pauses. "It is darkest winter and let us weep with those who weep. Let us share our strength so that we may salve our weakness. Let us be vessels of the Holy Spirit. Let us think of our friend, Mr. Griffin, and thank him with our spirits for what he has done for us."

"Amen," some of us say, not quite in sync.

"Thank you," Serenity says and slips into a sleep which we hope will heal him, to the extent that sleep can heal the mind's assault on itself.

It is just us again.

Emily suggests, "Let's go back to my apartment and exchange gifts." I hadn't seen any gifts but mine on the mantel, but everyone agrees to Emily's suggestion, with remarkable enthusiasm for this group. There may have been a huzzah.

Back at Emily's apartment, the dense civilized festivity—the books, the cloisonné tea set, the arrayed food, the evergreen boughs sprinkled with holiday lights, the curated second-hand furniture—contrasts with the paleness of Serenity's hospital room. Whatever we are doing feels like a party again.

Next to my presents are four presents. Not the twenty or so I'd expected the group to exchange with each other. Each present is long and flat and wrapped loosely, albeit in four very different kinds of wrapping paper.

"Okay," announces Emily. "We knew that our friend Duane was going to get us presents because that's who he is. And we wanted to acknowledge that, so each of us has brought a present for you," she says, turning toward me. She gestures toward me. I pick out my gift for Porter and hand it to him.

He opens the package with the blue-and-yellow baseball and exclaims, "This is wonderful! This brings me back to summer days in my youth. Thank you," he says and shakes my hand.

Then he hands me a package; it is soft beneath the wrapper. Work gloves.

I hand Jenny, Trevor and Emily their gifts and they hand me mine—mittens, everyday gloves, and dress gloves.

"Oh my God," I say. "This is great."

What I meant was "Oh my God, there are very few times in one's life when one feels truly seen and known and valued. And this is one of them."

We all hug each other one by one, and awkwardly: Emily puts her head on my chest and I thank her for the party and the gifts and the friendship and then Porter calls me a brother and I almost cry because I know what that term means to him and Jenny and I improvise a cursory friendly embrace and Trevor and I negotiate in a few micro-moments whether there should be a hug at all or just a hand-shake. I go for a full dad hug, quick but fierce with a back pat at the finish.

"We do need to get together again," Emily says.

"Yes," says Porter. "We need to know Mr. Griffin's fate."

"I can call his sister."

"Please let us know," says Jenny as she is walking out.

"I will."

"Do you need any help cleaning up?" asks Trevor. The kid's man-ners amaze me. I suspect he will eventually straighten up and go to college out of sheer politeness.

"Oh, no, I'm fine. But thank you, Trevor."

"Thank you for the gloves!" I say, brandishing the packages, but by then Jenny was outside of the building and Porter was outside of the apartment.

Emily closes the door behind us. Trevor turns left, waves and smiles wanly. I wave back and turn right. We disperse.

EMILY

I know we're all supposed to live in the present, and I've actually gotten a little better at it, but as I stepped into my apartment and saw the buffets of Vietnamese and Greek food and the half-full glasses and small plates and the gift from Duane, I thought: Thank you, **past tense.** Thank you for your brimming emotion and spent anxieties. The past tense does not know fear, because it knows "what has happened has happened." The past tense knows the joy of "I have." It knows it will be alright and even if it is not alright it will be done. I am sure I will sprout a regret or two soon. And, yes, I will have to clean this shit up. But now, tired, alone, done with my obligations, I look at my apartment and it shines.

PORTER

Driving home from that detoured Christmas party, I notice that the tears forming in my eyes multiply the Christmas lights of Grand Avenue. I pull the car over and sob, realizing that I am loved.

CODA

The next morning the weather is very cold—below zero—and the sun is very bright. The sky is comically blue; the sun, cartoonishly yellow. Franny is in the kitchen, which smells of coffee and toast.

I drink coffee and look out the window at the back yard. It is pure white snow surrounded by a high fence, backed by the random planes of garage and house and the fuss of winter trees.

There is a concept in design called negative space. Negative space is the part of the page you do not fill. Its blankness allows what is on the page to stand out more vividly. It is typically hard to convince clients of the value of this space. They want to fill it up with coupons or "sell copy" or another product photograph. This is not unreasonable; they bought the space. But when you succeed in keeping the page uncluttered and clean, what is left on the page ignites.

I think of this because I am staring at Franny's snow-covered backyard. A bird on a wire wobbles and catches himself.

I ask, "Are there birds in Minnesota in late December?"

She answers, "Yes, there are some. Not many, but some."

"This guy looks like he missed the bus."

"What?"

"Well, when he landed, he kind of slipped and righted himself. It looked like he didn't want anybody to see."

"Well, that didn't work out so well."

"He looks awkward. Can birds be awkward?"

"Why not?"

"Because they're in nature and isn't nature elegant?'

"He's a guy trying to do the right thing and not quite nailing the landing."

At that point, the phone rings. It is Pooch's firm. As the head of Human Resources introduces herself to me, I see Franny look out the window and smile. The bird is apparently singing.

I, on the other hand, fear he might be singing the ancient song of his species, "I could screw this up. I could screw this up. I could screw this up."

.

KEVIN FENTON is the author of *Merit Badges*, which won the AWP Prize for the Novel and the Friends of the American Writers Award, and *Leaving Rollingstone*, which Patricia Hampl called "the most important memoir to come out of the Midwest (or anywhere) in years." He works as an advertising writer and creative director; in that capacity, he's published essays in the design quarterlies Émigré and Eye (London), the anthology Looking Closer 2: Critical Writing On Graphic Design, and the UX design blog Boxes and Arrows. He got a slightly better education than he deserved at Beloit College, the University of Minnesota Law School, and the University of Minnesota MFA program. He lives in St Paul with his wife Ellen and his greyhound Evie.